This book is a work of fiction. Any references to historical events,
real people, or real locations is used fictitiously. Other names, places,
events, and characters are the product of the author's imagination, and
any resemblance to actual events or persons, living or dead, is entirely
coincidental.

Cover image by Kate Ulitin (Katyau), Vectorstock.

For Marston and Rachel.
Your encouragement was priceless.

Love Among Pigeons

ABRIA MATTINA

8 September, 2012 8:58 PM
From: Frank Kirk
To: Henrietta Kirk
Subject: RE: hi honey

Hi Mom, Dad

Sorry it's taken me three days to reply. Been busy. Accidents tend to go up around holidays, so...

I booked the entire Thanksgiving weekend off work. Willa will be home from school for the weekend, and I was wondering if you guys wanted to join us here. It would be nice to get the family together again.

Let me know what your plans are. I can pick you guys up at the airport or train station, if you decide to come. Hope you can make it. I'd really like it if we could do this.

Love,

Frank

1.
Reservations

Willa

"You have the hands of a child."

"Still not over that, are you?" I look at my hand, resting on the back of Jem's. It does look ridiculously tiny. "This comparison is unfair. You have long fingers."

He kisses my ear. "You like my long fingers."

I weave my fingers through the spaces between his knuckles and squeeze. They may be different sizes, but our hands match. Perfect for holding, as they are, the matching scars as souvenirs of where we've been.

Jem wraps an arm around my waist and gently tugs me out of my chair, onto his lap. He buries his face in my hair and nuzzles my neck. I just pull my book across the table and resume studying while he goes about his business. This part of the library is relatively deserted, but I've never been a fan of PDA.

Jem has been increasingly affectionate lately. It happens every time he goes for more blood tests, as if he's suddenly been reminded to seize the day.

"You switched shampoos," he accuses softly.

"It's *your* shampoo, remember?" It seems terribly cliché to keep another set of my toiletries at my boyfriend's place, so when I spend the night I use his soap.

"I like that floral crap you use." He rests his chin on my shoulder and pouts.

"I'll use the floral crap tonight."

"No, you're staying over tonight."

"I have class at eight tomorrow."

"And I have this nifty thing called an alarm clock."

I shake my head, smiling. "You hate being woken up early."

"I hate falling asleep without you." Jem places a kiss on the back of my neck.

"You say that now…"

"Stay," he murmurs. "I have it on good authority that I give awesome cuddles."

I don't validate this by replying. I believe Jem has all the evidence he needs. We drift into silence. I plan a menu for my next workshop, and Jem plays with my hair. He should be studying, but his mind is elsewhere. One more midterm for him, and then Thanksgiving weekend begins.

"Are you almost done?" He must want to get out of the library, and honestly, I could use the break. I shut my notebook.

"Let's eat dinner at your place."

⤙⤚

Jem's dorm room is a single. When he requested it, I assumed he wanted to hide his scars from others, but he set me straight with a whisper in my ear "I want to be able to take your clothes off whenever I want, and not worry about some other guy walking in." He makes a very good point.

We eat dinner on the bed because it's the closest thing he has to a couch. After, Jem reclines and cuddles me into the crook of his shoulder.

"Are you tired?"

"No," he says around a yawn. Jem kisses the top of my head. "I have something for you." He reaches into his pocket and pulls out a little piece of metal. "I saw it in the Market and thought of you."

It's a little silver ring with two perched birds in relief.

"They're pigeons," Jem announces.

I raise an eyebrow. "You mean rats with wings?" He rolls his eyes.

"Pigeons mate for life."

"Oh." That makes them slightly less repulsive…but only slightly.

He slips it onto my third finger. "I'd like you to think of it as a promise ring."

"Oh. *Oh.*"

As if he expected that response, Jem laughs at me. "You said yes to a bald stick figure, but a ring with birds on it makes you nervous?"

"Well, they *are* pigeons…" The thought of being with Jem for the long haul doesn't actually unnerve me. To be honest, I just accept it as a given that we will be together until one of us is no longer breathing. And whoever dies first will haunt the living one to prevent loneliness from setting in.

"I thought about getting you a Claddagh ring, but this seemed more… us."

"You mean weird?"

"Same difference."

I lean up towards him for a kiss. Jem looks so content right now.

"I was worried it wouldn't fit," he says. He picks up my hand and turns it back and forth, inspecting the ring. "I forgot to account for your child-sized hands when I bought it."

"Lucky break."

"Will you wear it?" He looks to me for reassurance. This happens sometimes—it suddenly seems to occur to him that we're together, and that life is fleeting. In those moments, it's important to affirm that we're in it together—that we want the same things out of life.

"Of course I will."

2.
Tastes

Jem

It's not being woken up early that I hate; it's letting Willa go. Here I am sleeping peacefully, cuddled up to someone warm and soft. Now I have to part with her before I'm ready to get up. But I do get to watch her dress, so it's not all bad.

"Let's become nudists," I say as she buttons her shirt.

Willa snorts. "I don't think nudist colonies take perverts like you." She leans down to kiss me goodbye. I try to pull her back into bed.

"I have to go."

"Lies."

I succeed in delaying her for a few minutes, but eventually, she works her way out of my death-grip cuddles. "I'll see you tonight."

"Be safe." I say it every day, and every day, Willa manages to come home with a new nick or burn.

She smirks. "What are the odds that I'll chop my hand in half twice?"

I'd rather not do the math on that one.

↔

I'm not worried about this midterm. It's for a required course that all first years take, Introduction to Essay Writing. It's where they unteach you everything you learned in high school English class. It's the kind of course you have to *try* to fail.

I'm just about to leave with nothing but a pen and my student ID when I get a text from Eric. The twit got locked out of his apartment, and his roommate won't be home for three hours.

Can I hang out at your place?

There are about a dozen coffee shops and student lounges between his place and mine, but pointing that out wouldn't do me any good.

Sure. I'll leave my door unlocked. Don't raid my fridge.

He's still in my room when I get back two hours later, stretched out on my unmade bed with an empty box of *my* crackers beside him.

"What? You said the fridge, not the cupboard."

"There's a café *in the lobby*."

"My wallet's at home."

I sigh. I can't justify sinking to his level just to argue about this. "Did you get in touch with your roommate yet?"

Eric shakes his head. "Still in class." I resign myself to a few more hours of having him in my space. I haven't packed for Thanksgiving weekend yet. While I grab a bag and start shoving clothes into it, Eric drinks my milk and flips through songs on my iPod dock. He lets about thirty seconds of each song play before he gets bored and switches it to something else.

"You cool?"

"Yeah."

It doesn't sound like he's being honest.

Without looking up from my iPod, he says, "Quick question. Uh, does it actually feel good to um…you know…in the butt?"

I give Eric a good long look. "Are you high?" It is simply implausible that my brother would ever ask about anal sex while sober.

"I'm not high. I was just curious…. So?"

"I wouldn't know," I reply in a never-ask-me-again tone.

Eric puts his hands up in surrender. "I'm not judging."

"What?"

His eyes go to my nightstand drawer, and he makes this awkward nodding motion. "I was looking for gum," he says by way of apology and explanation. Oh, Jesus. I know what he saw. There's a toy in there. And a harness.

"It's not for *me*."

Eric frowns, looking perplexed. "You mean Willa? But you're…equipped." His nod in the direction of my crotch is completely unnecessary.

"I know," I say through clenched teeth. Eric fidgets with his hands and I know he's itching to open that drawer again and take another look. "You're not cheating on her, are you?"

"No!"

"It's a size thing, isn't it?"

It's a bloody fucking miracle my brother doesn't get punched in the face on a regular basis. The guy has no verbal filter.

"It's a nerve damage thing." I might as well tell him before he gets carried away imagining things. "Some skin never regained full sensation after treatment ended."

"Oh. Shit, dude. I'm sorry, I didn't think of that."

"Clearly."

I know he's trying to be helpful when he suggests Viagra, but I'm really not in the mood to entertain advice. "I can get it up," I snap. "Most of the time I can't come from *normal* sex, so we do things that make us both feel good. No drugs. Got it?"

"Got it." He surrenders with a quick nod. I open my mouth to ask him to leave, but Eric isn't done running his mouth yet. "I didn't realize you were still paying for all that treatment. Cancer already cost you so much... So much time, so much dignity." His tone is sympathetic, but it doesn't make me want to punch him any less.

"You think I don't have dignity because of how I fuck my girlfriend?"

"That came out wrong."

"You don't say?"

"I'm sorry. I didn't mean to be a dick."

I don't tell him it's all right, or that he's forgiven, but I have the sense to keep my mouth shut. I throw some more stuff in my bag, focusing on staying calm and tryingl not to let this get to me.

"You okay, man?"

"I think you should go. Wait for your roommate in the lobby or something. I don't care."

3.
Menus

Willa

I head to Sasloves in the Byward Market after class. I promised Frank that I'd bring him some bacon sausage. He seemed unduly excited about it when we talked on the phone, even after I made a crack about phallic foods.

On the way to Sasloves, I pass by the fresh produce stalls and artisan craft booths. Most of it is just kitsch to attract the tourists, but there are some rare good finds to be had. On my way to the butcher shop, I see a sign that looks familiar. It takes me a second to place it: it's the symbol on the maker's mark inside my pigeon ring. The guy behind the table has a tray of tools in front of him. He's creating jewelry on the street. A poster declares that he does custom pieces, and there's a catalogue of designs. The only pre-made items in his booth are key chains and figurines constructed from cutlery.

Jem didn't just see the pigeon ring when he was passing through the Market. He put some thought into this. Trust Jem Harper to make a romantic gesture that ends with a winged rodent.

I send him a text: *I love you.* He's quick to reply: *Come over. I want to see you.*

~❧~

"I need to pack." Our train leaves in a little over an hour, and my suitcase is still empty. I lie on Jem's narrow bed, staring up at the yellowed ceiling. His head rests on my chest, where it's been since he gave up on having an orgasm. He wouldn't let me finish him off like we usually do, either. It weirded me out a little, his insistence on the kind of sex we almost never have. I didn't know what to say when it didn't pan out.

Jem turns his head to look at me. "Can I come with you?"

"Yeah." Standing up, I start sorting through the pile of clothes on the floor and look for my bra.

"Well, don't jump out of bed or anything," he grouches. I think his pride is a little bruised.

"We're running short on time," I remind him gently and lean down to kiss him. Jem cops a halfhearted feel before I put my bra back on.

Ten minutes later, we're out the door and headed to my place. He holds my hand for the entire walk and kisses the back of my head while I unlock my door. "Cuddle withdrawal?" I guess. We didn't spend much time doing that, after sex.

"You can make it up to me on the train." Jem sits down on the bed and looks at my empty suitcase, propped open against the dresser. "Oh, good, you're almost done."

"Shut up." I gather the basics and throw them in—change of clothes, pajamas, apron. The majority of my luggage space is devoted to jars of preserves and plastic containers of food.

"You bringing the whole pantry with you?"

"Pretty much." I have big plans for this Thanksgiving. It's

the first time that I'll get to cook for my family since I've been to culinary school. I can't wait to roll out some new tricks.

I arrange my clothes between the containers to provide cushioning and reach for my jacket.

"I love you." He looks sad, as though he truly needs to hear me say it back.

I sit down on Jem's lap and wrap an arm around his shoulders. "I love you too, forever and unconditionally."

His arms cradle me tightly while he places kisses on my collarbone. "Thanks," he murmurs.

"Do you want to talk about it?"

"Not really." I think sometimes he means 'yes' when he says that, but at the moment I'm confident that he actually doesn't want to discuss it. We don't have time for a heart-to-heart anyway.

Jem's phone rings. It's his dad. I go back to packing while he answers. I can hear Dr. Harper ask about the results of a test, and Jem tells him, "Not yet." He only finished writing midterms today. Why would he have his results back already?

It sounds as though Dr. Harper is saying that he's going to call someone, and Jem thanks him as if he genuinely means it. Jem's parents usually don't put this much pressure on schoolwork when it's just a midterm. I wonder what they'll do during final exams.

"Love you too. Bye." Jem hangs up and pockets the phone.

"I can't believe he's asking about your test results already. Does he think the prof is a magician?"

Jem looks as if he doesn't know what I'm talking about. "You're talking about exams," he says after a moment, clearly pleased that he figured it out. Jem points to his phone. "He was talking about blood tests."

"Oh, shit. I feel stupid."

Jem chuckles and runs a hand through my hair. "When you assume…," he says solicitously, probably expecting me to fill in the rest of the maxim.

"It wasn't an assumption. It was a reasonable deduction based on the evidence at hand."

"Well, then you're a pretty lousy eavesdropper, aren't you?"

"Shut it." I lean on my suitcase and zip it up. "Come on, we're gonna be late."

⌭

Eric is already at the train station when we arrive. Celeste dropped him off, and they've staked out a whole bench for making out.

Jem tilts his head as if he's watching the mating of a foreign species. "Is this how douchebags say goodbye?" he wonders aloud. We're close enough for Eric and Celeste to hear him, but they ignore the comment. "It looks like she's trying to eat his soul."

"Be nice."

Jem huffs. Five times, he's bet on when Eric and Celeste would split, and five times ,I've taken his money. He's the victim of his own wishful thinking. I try not to get involved. Otherwise, I might waste time wondering how Celeste manages to look so polished and made up at all hours of the day and night. Seriously, it's not normal to look anything other than haggard and frumpy by Friday afternoon.

They come up for air, and Celeste narrows her eyes at Jem.

"What are you staring at?"

"When does the stripping start?"

She flips him off and goes back to kissing Eric, who shrugs and accepts her affection for what it is. They'll only be apart for three days, but every couple handles separation differently.

They continue to make out until the last call for our train is announced, and Eric finally boards. He takes the seat across from Jem and me, and waves to Celeste until we've left the station behind.

"I wish we still lived in Ottawa," he says. He wouldn't have to leave Celeste on holidays if his family was still based there. While I have to admit that Smiths Falls is small and kind of boring, I wouldn't have met Jem if he lived in Ottawa.

"Christmas," Jem says tersely. "Stay with Grandma and Grandpa. Problem solved." This closes the matter for him. He puts in one ear bud and hands me the other.

"What's up his ass?" Eric asks me. I shrug because it's none of Eric's business, but the look Jem gives him is positively murderous. Normally, this would be the start of an argument, but Eric gets this weird, uncomfortable look on his face.

"Think the dining car is open?" he says, and gets up before either of us can answer.

"That was weird."

Jem cranks the volume on his iPod. "Ignore him."

⚘

Ivy picks us up at the train station and drops me off at Frank's house before heading home. All the lights are out already. It's weird, being back in the world of non-student people who have responsibilities before the crack of dawn. I suppose this is what people mean by 'a decent hour.' No wonder Frank is already in bed.

"I'll see you tomorrow." I lean over to kiss Jem goodbye. We've got plans to meet up for dinner since we won't see each other on Sunday. Family obligations demand otherwise.

"Text me when you're up." As if we don't already do that every day.

"Playlist?"

"Tracy Chapman, Fast Car."

"Said the Whale, Loveless."

Eric snorts. "You two are such dorks."

I step out of the car and lean down next to his window. "Did I mention I have a small supply of bacon sausages?"

His eyes widen and his nostrils flare. "I take back anything bad I ever said to you."

"Damn straight."

"So these sausages—"

"Soon, Eric. Soon."

I tiptoe through the front hall, trying not to make any noise. The ground floor smells like cooked beef. Frank probably seared a steak and ruined the frying pan in the process.

I find the pan in a sink of soapy water. It's not as bad as I thought it was, but it's not good either. I put it back in the sink when the plates catch my eye, specifically, the fact that there are two of them. Frank had company tonight.

Then I hear it, the subtle shift in the floorboards as a bed moves overhead. Frank's bedroom is above the kitchen.

Oh. Ohhh. Well, this is awkward.

I wonder if he forgot that I was coming home tonight. The Frank I know doesn't even hold Doug's hand when anyone else is around. Unless, that isn't Doug up there with him. I'm strangely bothered by the thought.

When things start getting uncomfortably *noisy*, I head outside and sit on the back patio. All right, so it's not a patio—it's some random paving stones and a lawn chair. And it's freaking freezing out here, but it'll do.

By the time I get to bed, it's past midnight. I don't even bother to change into pajamas. I just plug in my headphones, hit the mattress, and say goodbye to another day.

When I wake up, Frank's bedroom door is closed. I assume he's still asleep, but when I go downstairs, he's already at the table with a bowl of cereal. Frank's eyes widen in surprise, and I *know* he forgot my train was due to arrive last night.

"When did you get here?"

"Around eleven." I reach for the coffee pot, but it's empty. "The fuck, bro?"

"I've given up coffee."

I give him a well deserved are-you-insane look. He does look a lot better than the last time I saw him, and he's eating a bowl of some high-fiber cereal that looks like rabbit pellets. He must be on a health kick.

I settle for caffeinated tea instead of coffee and pour myself a bowl of cereal—the sugary kind that rots your teeth and contains mere micrograms of nutrition.

"Were you tired when you got in? Did you go to bed right away?" Frank stares at me probingly. I know what he's getting at.

"You need a sturdier bed frame."

Frank scrubs a hand over his face. "God, you heard?"

"Relax. I hear it's only gay if you make eye contact."

Frank doesn't seem amused. I put my hands up in surrender. "Just trying to make light. I have no intention of bonding with you over our shared love of penis."

Frank winces. "You know, I put a lot of mental energy into pretending that you're still innocent. Don't ruin that for me."

"I shall respect you delusions," I say with as much diplomacy as I can muster.

Conversation turns to plans for Thanksgiving. Frank bought a turkey, and it's defrosting in the fridge. Our parents are arriving in Brockville by train this afternoon. Doug is eating dinner at his dad's house tonight, since his grandma made a trip to Port Elmsley for the occasion. He can't blow off grandma.

"Jem's coming for dinner tonight."

Frank nods. "Doug is going to try to be here for dinner on Sunday. It depends if he can get away."

I met Grandma Thorpe, once. She's the kind of woman you don't say 'no' to. She'd sooner break a wooden spoon across your ass than give up an inch of control.

"I hope he can come," I say.

Frank doesn't reply. It's a complicated thing, wanting to include Doug in family gatherings. It would require Frank to do some explaining, and oh, how he hates explaining himself.

We eat in silence for a while. I can feel Frank's eyes on me, but he doesn't speak. When I glance up, he's staring at the pigeon ring. Why is he staring? It's a piece of jewelry. It's not like I never wear little decorations from time to time.

"That's a funny looking engagement ring," he says.

Oh. It wasn't the ring he was staring at; it was the finger I wear it on. Frank is clearly waiting for me to refute his assumption.

"They're pigeons."

He chews his cereal very slowly, with a thoughtful look on his face. "Pigeons."

"Yeah."

"You bought a ring with a bird that's good for absolutely nothing but shitting on cars?"

I've got to hand it to Frank—he's getting better at impersonating our dad.

"Actually, Jem bought it for me."

Frank's eyes narrow in a shrewd 'aha' moment. "He bought you a ring."

"Yes. But it doesn't shit on cars. Not that I'm aware of, anyway."

"Are you guys…" Frank makes a vague hand gesture. "…planning something?"

"Yes. Our goal is to invade Greenland by next year."

"Willa." It seems I've exhausted this little game.

"It's a promise ring."

For a moment, Frank looks stumped. "Is that like a purity ring?" He sounds so hopeful that I burst out laughing and narrowly avoid squirting milk out my nose.

"No. It's like an engagement ring, but without the pressure to plan a wedding immediately."

"Oh." I can't tell how Frank feels about that. As if the conversation never happened, he turns back to his cereal and munches in quiet contemplation. I'll take that as a sign that he's cool with it.

Suddenly he says, "Doug is living here now."

"No way. I thought all the furniture magically doubled." I point to the second couch and armchair wedged into the living room. Frank mutters something about being a smart ass.

"Have you told Mom and Dad yet?" As far as I know, they've never had a conversation about Frank's romantic life. Either they know and aren't saying anything before he does, or they honestly believe that he's celibate.

"I'll pay you fifty bucks to tell them."

I laugh, but Frank doesn't flinch. He' doesn't seem to be kidding. "You're such a wimp."

I kick him under the table and he kicks me right back.

"How long have you guys been together?"

It occurs to me how strange it is that I don't know this.

Frank tries to hide "eleven years" behind a cough.

"*Eleven* years? How do you have a relationship for more than a decade and not come out to your parents?"

"It was easy. They were used to having Doug around because we were friends as kids. I just never told them when things changed."

"Do you think they know?"

Frank shrugs. He looks both happy and worried. If they do know, he doesn't have to explain his relationship and his silence. If they don't, he has to explain his relationship and *eleven freaking years* of silence.

"Make it a hundred."

"What?"

"Dollars. Gimme a hundred bucks and I'll tell them for you."

"I wasn't serious."

I hold out my hand. "We both know you were."

Frank glances at my hand and smirks condescendingly. "Sorry, I don't keep hundreds stashed in my bathrobe."

"You can pay me later."

I get up to clear my bowl. Frank shakes his head slightly, still smirking. I think the idea of paying me to come out amuses him.

"What would you say to them?" he asks.

I pause to clear my throat. "I would say, bBeloved parents… Gotta lay it on thick, y'know? It is my great pleasure to inform you that your favorite son is very much in love with someone quite special.'"

Frank rolls his eyes.

"… and he's also an incurable cocksucker." I narrowly dodge the spoon he whips at my head.

4.
Breakfast

Jem

Mom lets us sleep in on Saturday morning. She has been very indulgent since we arrived, even putting fresh sheets on the beds and letting us order pizza last night. This is the third Thanksgiving we'll spend in this house, and the first one without a visit from Grandma and Grandpa. We're going to try to make a turkey. That'll be interesting. It'll probably also result in a 50/50 chance of food poisoning.

It's the first time Eric and I have been home since school started, and in honor of the occasion, Dad has decided to make pancakes. Color me surprised. He makes a double batch, but they're almost gone by the time Elise drags her ass out of bed.

Elise plunks down in the seat next to me, still in pajamas and staring vacantly like a zombie. She doesn't take any food but pours coffee into the cereal bowl-sized mug that Mom set out for her. She drinks about half the cup before she turns to me with something resembling humanity in her eyes.

"Are you the good twin or the evil twin?" I ask.

"Super-mega-ultra-evil triplet."

I think today is going to be a good day. She's not usually that quick-witted until she's had a full cup. I slide a pancake onto her plate. She douses it with coffee instead of maple syrup and digs in.

5.
Gratuity

Willa

Doug sleeps in. By the time he comes downstairs, I'm making the stuffing for tomorrow. He appears to be quite at home here. Waltzing in, he kisses Frank good morning as if PDA is no big deal for them and hugs me hello.

"That smells fantastic." He tries to take a piece of butter-soaked bread.

I slap his hand away from the bowl. "You can have some with dinner."

He tries giving me the puppy eyes, which get him no-where. Turkey stuffing is serious business. We ration it in this family.

"You *are* eating dinner here tomorrow, right?"

"I'll try my best." He does a good job of making it look easy, as if being a part of our family gatherings is something that he's been doing for years. It's the first time I can remember him being around for a holiday meal—Doug always had obligations to his own family. It's kind of a milestone.

"Is this dinner gonna be crazy fancy now that you're in culinary school?"

I snort. "Hardly."

Thanksgiving dinner is not the time to pull out fine dining recipes. 'Tis the season for old standbys, though I fully intend to add a bit of panache to them.

"Good," he says, smirking. "I was worried you'd turn into a snob and start pronouncing *chinois* correctly."

"Shut up, you hipster."

He's grown a scraggly beard since the last time I was home and has foregone his contacts this morning. The geeky thick-framed glasses are almost more douchey than the beard. Doug is *so* not meant to have a beard. His hair is dark but his skin is pale, and the contrast emphasizes his plasma tan.

"I was going for *tortured writer*," he says.

"Have you written anything?"

"He writes grocery lists," Frank interjects. "The bitter, tortured kind with shit like kale on them."

"Look at you two, ganging up on me."

This is how I know that Doug enjoys having me home, even though I've been a bit of a shit disturber in the past. His approval feels good because this is his home now too. It feels like things are finally settling into the way they should have been all along.

Doug heads over to his dad's house to visit with Grandma Thorpe. Frank goes out to run a few errands before everything closes for the holiday. I'm just cleaning up from my stuffing prep when he comes back with an envelope of cash in his hand. I take it before he can change his mind. Besides, how hard can coming out be?

I trust Frank, but just to annoy him, I count the money. "This is a hundred and fifty." Our agreement—if it can be called that—was for a hundred.

"I need you to tell them something else, too."

"What?"

Frank licks his lips, stalling. "I'm married."

Interlude
May 2001

Frank

"I found the perfect spot."

Doug is an optimist and has found a dozen such 'perfect' spots to hike over the years. I have to admit that they're all pretty spectacular but not what I'd call perfect.

On Saturday morning, we pack up our gear and head out for a hike along the creek. We usually go around the boggy area about twenty minutes away from the road, parting company from the creek until we can meet back up with it on the other side of the wetland. But today Doug goes through the bog, leaping from dry spot to dry spot. The ground sinks nearly half a foot with each jump. We can't rely on low branches or tree trunks to grab on to either. Most of these trees are dead, and their branches are brittle.

"Why can't we just go around?" I ask, breathless.

"Where's your sense of adventure?" He gives me that smile that's simultaneously heart-melting and soul-crushing. The bastard has no idea what he does to me.

We usually meet up with the stream where it's wide and shallow. In summer, the water level is so low that we can walk across it and not get our socks wet. A little further along, there's a bend in the creek where a small, pebbly beach has formed. I doubt we'll make it that far today because I'm already winded from all the leaping and bounding.

"We didn't even know this was here," Doug says.

At first, I can't see what he's talking about, but he keeps pointing until I get it. There's a rock formation on the edge of the marsh. Water funnels through the narrow gaps in the stone, feeding the creek.

"So that's where it begins again?"

"Just wait. It's amazing."

At the bottom of the rock formation, a short waterfall has eroded the creek bed to create a little pond. On the far side, the creek resumes its gentle flow.

"Perfect swimming hole, am I right?" Doug is beaming.

"Yeah, actually." The hole under the waterfall is about fifteen feet wide and ten feet deep. With the sun overhead, I can just make out the bottom.

Doug slips off his shoes and pulls his t-shirt over his head.

"You didn't tell me we were swimming. I didn't bring a suit."

He gives me a shit-eating grin. "You need one, Princess?"

I keep my mouth shut, but I'm annoyed. I can't swim naked with Doug. I can hide how much I like him in swim trunks, but not if we're both naked.

He's down to his boxers now.

"You're keeping your underwear on, right?"

Doug gives me a quizzical look.

Shit.

We've seen each other without clothes before but only in locker rooms, where anything more than a passing glance at another guy is unacceptable.

Doug steps up and takes the hem of my t-shirt in his

hands. "Don't be such a chickenshit." The words are nothing that he hasn't said to me a hundred times or more, but his tone is different. It's almost a whisper, like a tender dare. The back of my neck starts to tingle, and I push away the idea that Doug is suggesting anything.

Doug lifts my shirt over my head and tosses it onto his pile of clothes. He's got this look in his eye—examining but not probing, inviting but not solicitous. He's like a bored predator that's too full to eat but takes stock of potential prey nonetheless. Maybe he does suspect something, and he's planning to call me out. I'm not sure I could survive the humiliation. I definitely couldn't stand to lose him. I can only keep Doug as a friend if I keep my mouth shut and my hands to myself.

He starts to undo my belt, but I replace his hands with mine before I get carried away. For a split second, he looks annoyed.

Without a word Doug turns around, pulls down his boxers, and leaps into the pool. The resounding splash quiets the nearby wildlife for a few seconds, and then the buzz starts up again.

Doug surfaces with a whoop. "Shit, it's freezing." He follows up that brilliant sales pitch with, "Get your ass in here!"

I take my sweet time removing my shoes, socks, and pants. By the time I'm down to my underwear, Doug seems tired of waiting. He pulls himself out of the pool while I study my toenails. I can't let him know that seeing him buck naked and dripping wet does things to me.

"Leave 'em on," he says. "You can go commando on the walk home." Then he does something very strange. He takes my hand.

I'm so surprised by the gesture that I don't realize until it's too late that he's pulling me into the water. We hit with a splash and sink until I can feel the silty bottom of the pool under my feet. Doug is still holding on to my hand. I'm about to kick off for the surface when something touches my face—my mouth—so lightly and quickly that for a moment I'm not sure it wasn't just a bubble rising. But it happens again, firmer this time, and lasts for the space of two heart-beats. That's a hand on the back of my neck.

Doug lets go. He beats me to the surface.

And the bastard lied. It's not freezing; it's fucking *arctic*. I take a gulp of air and blurt out the first thing that enters my head. "Jesus Christ, we'll be lucky not to lose our nuts to frostbite."

There's a second of hesitation before Doug laughs…too loudly. He looks like somebody who just got pinched him in a sensitive spot, but is trying not to admit it hurt.

I don't know what to do here. What is he playing at? Is he trying to make an ass out of me, or did he mean to do… that? We tread water, watching each other for some signal that this is okay or that we should do something. I try not to let my eyes stray lower.

"Are you okay?" he asks, finally.

"I'm fine." Confused and insecure, but physically fine. Maybe that was his idea of a prompt to come out, as if I'd spill my guts that easily. I put the question to him. "Are you okay?"

That look of disappointment is back. Without a word, Doug swims to the edge of the pool and hauls himself up onto the rock.

"Where are you going?" The only answer I receive is a

vague hand gesture, brushing me off. Doug grabs his shoes and underwear, nothing else, and heads off into the trees.

What the hell just happened?

I pull myself up onto the rock. It's harder now that my limbs are so cold. Doug has a twenty-meter head start, so I just grab my shoes and head after him.

This part of the forest is secluded between the wetland and the curving creek. There's only so far he can go without crossing water again. I find him on the pebbly beach, watching the creek pass by with his hands on his hips. I see from here that his shoulders are tense, and for a moment, I consider the possibility of not approaching him.

I'm no good at this. He was obviously expecting me to say something back there to confirm that I like guys—that I like him more than I should.

"Can we just forget this happened?" he says when he hears me coming up behind him. He sounds completely miserable.

I shuffle my feet, feeling stupid. "What was that back there?"

"Nothing. It was stupid," he says sullenly. "Forget it."

"It was nice." I didn't mean to say that. I shouldn't have said that. Jesus…

"Nice?" he sounds disbelieving. "Really?" There's a note of hope in his voice, as if he actually wants me to say yes.

It clicks. He wasn't trying to corner me into coming out. He was making a move. That's what it was, right? And I didn't respond. Fuck. I should have said something. I shouldn't have made him feel bad.

I take a few steps closer to him. He stiffens. "I'm sorry I suck at this." It's a little easier to apologize to the back of his head.

Doug turns his head a fraction of an inch, so I'm just visible out the corner of his eye. "You're not mad?"

"I'm not mad."

Doug swallows. "So… what are you?"

"Inexperienced." I take the risk of looking like an idiot and lean forward to kiss the corner of his mouth. It's a new thing, the way it reacts against my lips.

He sighs. His hand finds mine. "Me too."

He didn't need to tell me that. I know how inexperienced my best friend is. I want to kiss him again, but when I lean in, he interrupts me. "I had this whole plan worked out, to find out if you liked me back. I thought you liked guys too, but I couldn't be sure."

A short laugh bubbles up from somewhere deep on my gut. "What was the plan?"

Doug smirks. "Doesn't matter. When it came down to the moment, I just thought I'd kiss you really fast before I chickened out."

"I like slow." Really, I have no idea what I like. I've only kissed twice, and both times were today.

Doug doesn't lean in for another kiss. He doesn't even face me. He just takes me by the hand and starts walking leisurely back to the place where we left our clothes.

"I meant slow kisses." As for taking a relationship slowly. I've imagined this for too long to waste any more time.

Doug laughs. "I know." But he doesn't try to kiss me again. I'm not sure what that means, but he's still holding my hand. That's important, right?

I look down at our joined hands and it occurs to me. This isn't just important; this changes everything.

6.
Service

Willa

First I punch him in the shoulder. *Then* I hug him and say congratulations.

"When did you do this?"

"About a month ago."

"Why didn't you tell me? Why didn't you *invite* me, damn it?" I can hear the shrill note in my voice but can't seem to pull it down a notch. Frank remains annoyingly calm, but I sense the condescension he tries to keep out of his voice.

"It wasn't some big show. We just went to the courthouse to get it done and out for dinner after."

"Pictures. You *must* have taken some." My brother, like a typical guy, took *one* picture. It's a cell phone pic. I can see why it isn't framed on his mantle.

"The marriage is more important than the wedding," he says, as if he's imparting one of the only good pieces of advice he has to give.

"I'm still gonna get you a wedding gift." A moment of inspiration hits me and I snap my fingers. "A can of WD-40 for your bed frame!"

It's my turn to get punched in the shoulder.

7.
Mise en place

Jem

I spend some time in the office with Mom, researching tips on roasting a turkey. Usually, Grandma spearheads the effort, but Mom insists that it can't be that complicated.

"Did you buy a pre-gutted turkey?" I ask, scrolling through a webpage about how to clean and gut a bird.

"I don't know. What does it say on the package?"

We figure out how long the turkey will need to defrost and that it does not need gutting after all. After some debate about whether we have to wash it or if that was done at the butcher shop, we settle on washing. We move on to the part about how to prepare and cook it, and Mom suddenly remembers that she doesn't own a roasting pan. Grandma always brought one with her.

"That seems like an important piece of equipment."

Mom gives me a look and tells me not to be a smart ass. "What's Willa's number?" she asks, reaching for the phone.

Mom puts the call on speaker before she asks Willa if it's possible to roast a turkey without a roasting pan. There's a pause, and I can tell that Willa might be wondering if Mom is being serious.

"How big is your turkey?"

"Twenty pounds. Would a baking sheet work?"

"No, the fluid would overflow the sides of the pan. You can roast it in casserole dishes if you cut it up first, but you wouldn't get any stuffing that way. Unless you pound the breasts flat and stuff them like chicken ballotine."

Mom and I look at each other. What the hell is chicken ballotine?

"But you would need toothpicks or twine for that, and three-to-four casserole dishes. It would reduce your cooking time slightly too. With a convection oven…"

And she has officially lost us.

Willa talks for a few more minutes about fluid ratios for ballotine stuffing and the number of turns we'd have to do. Apparently, we'd have to skin the turkey, poach it, and then somehow put the skin back on. By the end of Willa's explanation, Mom looks a little stunned.

"Thank you for your help, Sweetie," she says to Willa.

"You're welcome. Call me if you have any problems."

Mom hangs up and looks at me. This is the moment to admit defeat. "Think the grocery store would have roasting pans?" she says.

"Probably."

"I'll get my keys."

8.
First Seating

Willa

Frank manages to wind himself up good and tight on the drive to Brockville. He copes with his nerves by micromanaging, and out comes a litany of rules regarding the Great Coming Out.

"You can't just blurt it out."

"Fine."

"And you can't use a word like faggot anything like that."

"Got it."

"And *don't* mention the squeaky bed frame."

"Can I mention that Doug's a moaner?"

Frank groans. "This is a bad idea."

"I'm just screwing with you. I'm not going to tell them anything obnoxious or be rude about it. I'm just gonna say it, and if they freak out, I'll act as a buffer. They're used to being pissed off at me."

We come to a red light, and Frank looks over at me. "You should really try to reconcile some of this… anger. It's Mom and Dad. They're the only parents you'll ever have."

Frank is the only person who might understand because it's his family too, but on this issue, we're miles apart.

"Tessa was the only firstborn they'll ever have." I can't give her back to them, nor can I go back in time and create the dignified, peaceful death they wanted her to experience.

"I think they'll like having Doug as a son-in-law," I say. "Remember how they gushed over Clay?"

He was the guy everyone thought Tessa would eventually marry—before she got sick, before that douchebag slipped away like a selfish coward. The bastard was only capable of loving her when loving was easy.

Frank grunts. "I remember."

He and I had a bonding moment over Clay—while keying his car. I bet if we told Mom and Dad that now, they wouldn't even be mad. There's no love left for Clay.

"Do you think things will change," Frank says, "once they know Doug's their son-in-law?" His tone is philosophical, but it's a legitimate question.

We really don't know how Mom and Dad will react to Frank coming out; none of their children have done it before. But they like Doug, and they're used to him because he's been hanging around since kindergarten. That fact alone makes me optimistic about this.

The train is late. We wait in the parking lot, leaning against the sunny side of Frank's car to soak up some vitamin D.

"How long do you think ViaRail would stay in business if they offered refunds to people more than thirty minutes late to their destination?"

Frank snorts. "Two weeks."

"You took the train a lot in college, didn't you?" It makes sense. He went to school in Cornwall, and Doug was at McGill in Montreal.

Frank nods.

"Either that or the Greyhound. I ate a lot of bad food out of vending machines."

"The things we do for love." I nudge Frank with my elbow. "Looks like he's got you eating well now, though."

Doug is a nutritionist. He splits his workweek between the nursing home and the health food store.

Frank closes his eyes and lets out a long, suffering sigh. "I am so sick of spinach." Like the rotten sister that I am, I laugh at him. "I feel like an alcoholic, hiding bottles all over the house. Except I'm hiding chocolate bars and chips."

"Take heart." I clap him on the shoulder. "I'm making pie for dessert, and he can't stop you from eating it because it's Thanksgiving tradition."

"Don't tell him you're baking pie." Frank shakes his head. "He'll insist you put fruit in it."

Though pumpkin and apple pies are typical Thanksgiving desserts, in the Kirk house it's tradition to eat chocolate peanut butter pie. And we use the sugary kind of peanut butter, none of that pure, organic crap.

The train finally pulls into the station with a loud rattle. Neither of us stands up to go inside. We'll wait for Mom and Dad to come out to the parking lot, like the chicken-shits we are.

Frank reaches over and picks up my left hand. He moves the pigeon ring one finger over so it's no longer on my ring finger.

"So they don't assume," he says.

"Hey, why don't you and Doug wear rings?"

"I don't wear one because I'd have to take it off for work, so it would be like spending the money for nothing. Doug just doesn't like rings." It's a surprisingly practical answer. I thought he would say *because everyone would know about us.*

"Are you out at work?"

He smirks at me. "Trying to increase your profit?"

As if I'd make him to pay me to come out to every person in town. "You couldn't afford me."

"I'm out to a few people," he says. "You know, HR people."

That makes me laugh. The only people who know about the marriage are the people responsible for putting them on their spousal insurance benefits. "Dude, you're married now. Time to own up."

Travelers begin to trickle out of the station. Frank straightens up to look for Mom and Dad at the very moment that I slouch down. He waves to them, and I wince.

We have an uneasy truce, my parents and I, which is predicated on a mutual understanding that we do not talk about Tessa. It sort of makes things difficult, since my formative years were spent in the orbit of Tessa and her cancer. Talking about her inevitably leads to dark questions, and to accusations and blames, so we just don't.

Mom and Dad look a little bleary. Maybe they slept on the train. They hug Frank, and I do this weird embrace with them that feels saturated with worry. That's a new one. It's usually suspicion and resentment.

Mom straightens my jacket collar. "Where's Jem?"

"The car only seats four." It's true, but I somehow manage to sound snotty by pointing that out. They must think I do this stuff on purpose. "He's coming to dinner tonight."

"Oh. Good."

"Does he still have that stupid haircut?" Dad asks, circling the car. He probably wants to be on the road already.

"It's shorter now, if that's what you mean." I cut it for Jem at Easter, but he hasn't let me trim it since, so it's sort of shaggy now. Dad's hair is looking a little unkempt too. It's almost entirely white now, and thinning at the crown. He's old before his time.

"You could use a trim," Mom says to me. "I think you've got split ends."

My mother has always struggled with my hair. Mine is curly, hers is dark and straight. When I was a kid she believed my hair was simply unmanageable.

Frank gives me a pleading look as he shuts the trunk on the suitcases. I think he's begging me not to deflect Mom and Dad's scrutiny by outing him here in the parking lot.

"It's okay," I mouth, and he relaxes a little. I slide into the backseat beside Mom. Dad is already fiddling with the tuner, trying to find a weather report. "It's sunny and warm. Don't question it."

"I want to know the five-day forecast." He's used to fickle Newfoundland weather. "I brought an umbrella, just in case."

Because we don't have those in Ontario.

Frank finally gets in and starts the car. Dad asks him if he thinks it's likely to rain this weekend, even though there isn't a single cloud in the sky. Frank manages to keep a straight face while he answers.

Show off.

"Well, I brought an umbrella just in case," he repeats. I look from him to Mom, both of them stubborn and set on their agenda, and realize that my parents are well on their way to becoming *old people*.

9.
Cocktails

Jem

Mom under-shot the size of the pan. We put the frozen bird in to compare size, and it barely fits.

"It's okay," Mom declares. "Turkeys shrink when you cook them. Right?"

"Right." But I'm pretty sure the parts that are touching the pan will stick and burn. I think air has to be able to flow around the turkey for it to cook evenly. I'm not sure. I tune out sometimes when Willa describes the minutiae of recipes.

"I think it'll be fine as long as there's enough room to get the baster down to the fluid at the bottom," Dad says.

Mom blinks at him as if he just said something in a foreign language. "Do we own a baster?"

We all start riffling through the kitchen drawers. Dad suggests using a large syringe, but we don't exactly have random medical supplies kicking around the house anymore.

Mom sighs. "Where are my keys?"

After Mom leaves, I head upstairs in search of Elise. A few months ago, she would have been interested in cooking the turkey, but I guess she's done trying to impress her boyfriend with food. I find her in her room, dressed up in a skirt and a nice sweater as if she's headed somewhere. Elise ignores me as she digs through her jewelry box, looking for something in particular.

"Where are you going?"

"I'm meeting Kipp."

"Your brothers are in town." We haven't seen each other in over a month, and she's taking off already?

Elise snorts. "Like I haven't had eighteen years to get sick of you two."

I go over to her jewelry box and pick up the little gold crucifix Mom and Dad bought for her years ago. "Here."

"Dude. Get away."

"Stand still." Despite her protests, I manage to get it on her without breaking the clasp. It's no chastity belt, but maybe it'll make her boyfriend hold off on touching her for a few seconds… or years.

"If I wear this, you can't give me shit for the rest of the day," she says.

"Fine." That's a promise I fully intend to break.

Elise turns back to the mirror and starts putting on make-up.

"What do you need that for? Doesn't this jackass think you're beautiful already?" My favorite way to see Willa is with her face bare and soft from sleep. Makeup is nice sometimes, but it isn't her.

"Don't call Kipp a jackass. And he's coming here for dinner tomorrow, so don't be a spazz."

"He's coming here on Thanksgiving Sunday? What about his family?"

"His parents don't believe in celebrating the oppression of Native Peoples. Plus they're vegetarians, so no turkey."

I can't believe she just equated those two things as reasons to visit us for dinner, and I can't believe the Lathams are such hippies.

"Has he ever offered you weed?"

"Why, you want some?"

"Elise…"

"I'm kidding. Weed gives me a stomachache."

That does not make me feel the least bit comforted because it means she has tried weed at some point. Where's the reset button that will make her go back to being an innocent little kid?

Elise leans in close to the mirror to put on mascara. I hate that she's getting so dolled up for this guy. It's barely two o'clock in the afternoon.

"Damn," she murmurs when a clump gets stuck in the corner of her eye.

"It's a sign. You better wash it all off."

"Be quiet."

I flop down on the bed, defeated, while Elise continues to apply a thick layer of paint that she doesn't need. I can't believe she feels the need to do that. Maybe this guy isn't treating her right, and the makeup is part of a self-esteem issue.

"Does the jackass tell you you're beautiful?"

"Call him that one more time," she dares me.

"Does he?"

"Yes."

"And do you believe him?"

"Can you just shut up? You're distracting me."

Yep, he's definitely a jackass. Maybe he says one thing and treats her in another way. Girls are good at picking up mixed signals and making it their fault.

I'll have to talk to Eric about a plan to torture this jackass tomorrow night. It has to be a coordinated effort since Elise will probably take Latham's side once we start ganging up on him.

On the other side of Elise's wall, I can hear Eric having a conversation with Celeste. They've been on the phone since breakfast ended. Three hours ago.

"He saw her yesterday. What could they have to talk about for that long?"

"They play online games together and coordinate over the phone," Elise says. "Celeste is into World of Warcraft and COD."

"Really?"

Elise giggles. "I know, right? I guess that's how she takes out her aggression."

"Then how does she still have so much bitchiness left over?"

My sister heaves a great sigh of annoyance. "I hope he gets bored of her soon," she says. "Problem is, they were friends before. He'd want to go back to being friends. She'd never go for that. It'd be the slow, poisonous kind of breakup because neither of them would want to be the one to call it quits."

Her candidness is refreshing. Elise defended Eric's relationship with that succubus in the beginning, but at the time, she was at the start of her own iffy relationship. She probably felt that she couldn't defend her own choices and simultaneously tear down someone else's. But now she's more secure, and her real feelings about Celeste are starting to come out.

Elise puts down her makeup and starts rummaging around for a pair of shoes. "I thought he'd bring her out of her shell a little, but she's just as stuck-up as before. She wouldn't even make s'mores with the rest of us on Labor Day because she didn't want to get chocolate on her manicure."

"You made s'mores without me?" My indignation is lost on Elise.

She starts crawling around the bed, riffling through the crap underneath. "Yeah, and she refused to eat the ones Eric tried to share with her because they were too *fattening*."

"I never thought Eric'd go for someone who's that high-maintenance."

"It's probably easier to launch a space program than keep up with her demands." Elise backs up from under the bed with a dusty shoe in hand. "She must be really, really good in bed."

"Gross, Lise."

"She takes medication, you know," Elise adds in a conspiratorial whisper. "I saw a bottle of Xanax in her purse once."

It's interesting to know that, but it makes me uneasy to hear my little sister talk about medication in such a judgmental way. Mental illness is invisible, but there are people who genuinely need meds to function.

"Anxiety isn't that uncommon, you know." It is difficult to imagine Celeste having a panic attack, though. She's always so pulled together and cold. Human weakness is beneath her.

"A lot of the girls on cheer squad popped Gravol like it was breath mints. Mellows you out."

"How do you know that?"

"Swim team," she says. "I was in the locker room when they were there, most of the time. I could tell you which girls would throw up after lunch, too."

"Thanks, but I'm good."

Elise pauses to text something, probably to the jackass,

and we're right back to the subject of Eric's relationship. "I actually think it's the religion issue that's going to pull them apart," she announces.

It's a likely conflict, but Elise is betting on the dark horse if she actually thinks that will be the catalyst to break them up. Eric has faith, and worse, religion. Celeste and her family are atheists, the defensive kind. It's the kind of thing that wouldn't become an issue unless they decided to get married or have kids.

"I have to go. I'm gonna be late." Elise grabs her keys and purse, and takes a second to pat her pockets in search of forgotten items. "I think that's everything. Oh, got any condoms I can borrow?"

My stomach lurches up into my throat. "What?!"

"Kidding." Elise sticks her tongue out at me and prances out the door.

I'll just sit here quietly having a heart attack, thanks.

Interlude
July 2001

Frank

I meet Doug at the hardware store after his shift ends. The sun went down about an hour ago, but the sky is still purple, with enough moonlight to navigate. We make our way to the park, to the little hutch at the top of the spiral slide and sit there together. Doug pulls me over so I'm sitting between his bent knees, my back resting against his chest.

"Missed you." I twine our fingers together and kiss the back of his hand. He smells like wood shavings. "I'm thinking of saving up for a car."

"Yeah?"

"Yeah." I smile. "Unless I can get someone to sell me a backseat by itself."

It makes me a little giddy, imagining the freedom and privacy a car would provide, what it would mean for our relationship. We've made out a few times, as often as we can find privacy, really, but despite the skinny-dipping stunt Doug pulled out in the woods, he hasn't let me get him out of his clothes since.

Sometimes he makes me paranoid. Doug loves to kiss, and he's good at it, but he's been slow to warm up to everything else. It makes me wonder if he's as interested in me as I am in him, and I feel like a creep whenever I push too far.

"I was thinking," Doug says.

"Mmm?"

"It's sort of the weekend." It's actually Tuesday, but teenagers don't get prime weekend days off from summer jobs. Doug and I both have the day off tomorrow.

"You want to sleep over?" he says.

Sleepovers are nothing new. Our parents probably won't bat an eye if we ask, but it's the first sleepover since we started dating.

"Sure." I turn my head and kiss his cheek. I'm feeling a little bold, so I add, "Should I bother to bring pajamas?"

Doug rests the bridge of his nose against my temple and sighs. His arms tighten around my middle. "Yes," he says, very deliberately. There's no flirting, and he sounds deeply uncomfortable.

I swallow. "Are you okay?" He's regretting this; I know it. He doesn't like me that way or like me as much as he thought he did. Maybe there's someone else, or maybe he told someone and they talked him out of being with me.

Doug shrugs. "It's all changing too fast."

"What is?"

"Us." He sees that I'm freaking out and places a placating kiss on my lips. "I thought we'd just… be best friends and love each other too."

"Isn't that what we're doing?"

He smiles like I've said something funny. "You can be pushy sometimes."

"Oh."

He brushes the tip of his nose against my ear. "It's like all you want is sex." We haven't had sex. We haven't done anything below the waist, except for a little dry humping, and that only happened once.

"I'm sixteen."

Isn't that reason enough to be horny all the time? Maybe it wouldn't be like this if I were with someone else, but Doug is just so damn appealing. Even his fingernails are perfect. Seriously, *fingernails*.

Doug snorts. "What am I, eighty?"

"It feels that way sometimes." I say softly, so it doesn't sound like I'm accusing him. The last thing I want is for Doug to pull back when we're only just beginning to figure out how this whole relationship thing works.

Doug doesn't reply. We're silent for a few minutes, but he lets me keep holding his hand. I stroke his thumb with my thumb, trying not to wish that it were an entirely different part of him.

"Do you still want to sleep over?" he asks.

"Do you want me to?"

Doug nods. His cheek brushes my scalp. "You make me nervous," he admits.

"I do? How?"

"You seem so sure."

I try not to panic, but I wonder if he means that he isn't sure about us. "You made the first move," I remind him.

"I did," he agrees. "I didn't know how it would turn out. I just knew I liked you."

I squeeze his hand. "I like you too." We've been best friends for as long as we can remember, and there's a form of love in that, but I wonder when we'll be able to say *I love you* and know that we're talking about something completely different.

Doug kisses my temple and says, "Let's go."

Part of me wonders if I should insist that we continue this conversation, but another part of me worries that if I did that, I would accidentally talk him into leaving me. So I keep my mouth shut and follow him out of the hutch, over to the tree where we left our bikes.

He takes the lead on the ride home. I watch his back as I follow behind, thinking about all the ways in which he's right; things have changed between us. Everything is different. And I don't know how things could ever go back to the way they were if we broke up.

⌁

As predicted, Mr. Thorpe doesn't suspect a thing when Doug asks if I can sleep over. "Keep it down," is all he says and wishes us goodnight.

There's a routine to sleepovers after so many years of friendship. We stay downstairs for an hour, playing video games. Luke comes through the living room to get a glass of water and stops to watch the game for a few minutes. No one says anything. Luke's eyes don't even flicker from the TV screen, and I take a chance by resting my foot against Doug's.

How does no one see it? I wonder. So much has changed in two months, and nobody has noticed. Sometimes, I feel like it's written on my forehead: *I love Doug Thorpe, and he's an amazing kisser.* But everyone looks at us like they always did, as though we're still two best friends, even when we're in the middle of a tense discussion about our romantic relationship.

"Can you show me how to beat the library?" Luke asks.

"Tomorrow," Doug replies. "It's late." Luke heads upstairs to bed, and twenty minutes later we shut off the game.

Doug reaches over and takes my hand. With the TV off, the living room is dark, and we just sit there for a moment, holding.

"Tree house or my room?" Doug whispers. The tree house offers more privacy, but I'm worried about making him uncomfortable.

"Your room."

We turn off the porch light, lock the front door, and make our way up to bed. The house is quiet as we wash up and unroll our sleeping bags. Doug doesn't go into the bathroom to change out of his clothes, which confuses me. I thought he wanted space for things to be like they used to for a little while. Yet he goes and does that.

I crawl into my sleeping bag, determined not to make anything of it. Doug turns off the light and joins me on the floor.

"Goodnight," he murmurs. Doug leans over me with one hand on my chest, and bends down to kiss me. It's tender, so I follow his lead. Doug breaks away just slightly and finishes the kiss with three short pecks.

He rests his forehead against mine and sighs. "Sometimes I like you too much."

My gut twists. What is that supposed to mean? The way he says it makes it sound bad, as if it's worse than not liking me enough.

Doug shakes his head slightly. "I dunno what to do."

I place my hand over the one he has on my chest. His palms are sweating.

"Doug?"

"I want you so bad it feels like I'm about to explode," he says, all in a rush so I can barely catch the words. "And then I come back down to earth and everything is changing too fast."

Jesus, that's what's wrong? I'll settle for being wanted too much any day of the week.

I tilt my chin up to kiss him. "Roll over."

Doug shifts onto his back, and I nudge him until he moves over onto his side. I'd like to touch him. I'd like to discover every part of him, all the unknown places that no one else has ever touched before. I'd like to kiss him everywhere, to learn the smell of his skin and hear him curse softly. And I want to know if he thinks about me in the same way and wants the same things. I think I understand what he means when he says he feels as though he might explode, but I can't be sure.

There's a lot we can't talk about, at least not yet.

I roll, so I'm lying close to him, curled around his back and against the backs of his legs. Spooning is simple. Spooning is comforting. I can romance my boy—prove to him that I love him, that it's not entirely about making each other hot.

I wrap an arm around his waist, and Doug lays his hand over mine.

"This okay?" I ask.

"Yeah," he replies. "This is perfect."

10.
Lunch

Willa

Jem is already at the house when we arrive. He barely lets me step out of the car before picking me up in a hug. It feels as if we've been apart for weeks instead of a day.

"Hello, Jem," Dad says.

"Hello, Mr. Kirk." They've given Jem permission to call them Gary and Henrie a few times now, but I warned Jem that it was a trap. They respect manners, and mannerly young men call their girlfriends' parents Mr. and Mrs., according to Gary and Henrie. They also believe that it's okay to call their daughter's boyfriend 'Jim' for the first six months, just to test what he's made of.

Frank goes to retrieve the luggage from the trunk and tosses his house keys to me. "Open the door for them. I'll be right behind you."

I smirk compulsively and Frank gives me a severe look. I can almost hear him willing me not to make an innuendo out of that.

"Sure, bro."

On the walk up to the front porch, Dad asks, "Is that street sign new?" He points to the *Road May Flood* notice at the far end of the block.

"No."

"I think it's new."

And *I* think that's the kind of random, stubborn, curmudgeon-y shit that old men say.

"Have there been floods lately?"

We've just had one of the driest summers on record. "Nope." I can't say any more than that without the risk of being sarcastic.

We step into the foyer and take off our shoes. It hits me when I bend to put mine on the rack that half of the shoes already there belong to Doug. We should've rehearsed explanations for a few things before we left for the train station. Such as why Doug's stuff is in Frank's house. Saying that they're roommates would be a plausible excuse, at least to people who haven't known Frank since he was born.

"Is that a new couch?" Mom looks from the plaid monstrosity Frank bought when he moved out to the beige leather sofa on the opposite side. We might be in luck. She doesn't recognize Doug's furniture.

Frank clears his throat. "Yeah, I'm uh... upgrading some things."

"That's great. You can't live like a college student forever."

"Are you ever going to paint the walls?" Dad asks.

"White goes with everything."

I offer to get drinks for everyone as Mom and Dad settle into the beige couch. Frank follows me into the kitchen.

"White goes with everything? Dude, you suck at being gay."

"Shush," he hisses. Frank grabs the jug of fresh strawberry lemonade out of the fridge and gives me a funny look when I tell him about the special ice cubes in the freezer. There are bits of strawberry, mint, and lemon peel frozen into them.

"I didn't know lemonade could be this fancy."

He has a point. We're a frozen-cans-of-Minute Maid kind of family. I start making sandwiches for lunch while he serves the lemonade. They seem to like it. Mom doesn't criticize, and Dad hasn't made an inane comment in almost five minutes.

Mom comes to see me just as I'm plating crab salad sandwiches and charcuterie. For a few seconds, she looks at the food, trying to figure out what's in it. She smiles at me. It's been ages since she did that. The expression doesn't reach her eyes, but the corners of her mouth are turned up. She's trying.

"You're learning lots at school?"

"Yeah, loads." I feel like I haven't had time to breathe these past two months. I'm learning so much so fast. My days are a blur of demos, practical classes, workshops, and the endless practice of new techniques at home.

"They're teaching you good recipes?"

In the other room, I hear Dad asking Jem about school. It's easier with Jem because he's getting a traditional education. I'm not.

"Cordon Bleu isn't so much about recipes. It's about proper techniques." It's no good to be able to execute a recipe perfectly if you can't create your own using flavor profiles and a wide range of cooking techniques. It represents the difference between being an automaton and being an artist.

Mom points to one of the bowls on the charcuterie platter. "What's that?"

"Pickled, spiced eggplant. Homemade." And it's damn good, if I say so myself. "The bocconcini is homemade too."

"The what?" I think it's the first time bocconcini has ever been served in this house. Growing up, we ate a lot of Kraft Singles.

I stab a slice of the pale cheese with a fork and hold it out to her. "Try it with something else on the plate. Bocconcini is bland and meant to be paired."

"The things you're learning…"

I start to describe how the fig compote is made, but her eyes start to glaze over the same way Jem's do when I get too technical about food. Sometimes, it's hard to accept that all people really want to know is if it's edible.

I hand her the bowl of crostini and zucchini chips and ask her to carry it into the living room. "The zucchini goes great with parsley mayo."

"I didn't know Hellmann's made parsley mayo."

It's kind of painful, hearing her say that. "They don't. See, you start with eggs…"

11.
Setting the Table

Jem

There's a golf game on that Mr. Kirk wants to watch. I can't understand the impulse to play golf, much less watch it, but he seems pretty serious about his interest. Maybe there's something special about this particular snore-fest. I mean... game.

Mr. Kirk even asks Frank if he can tape the game during dinner. Frank suggests using the PVR recorder, but Mr. Kirk insists on a tape so he can take it home and watch it in case he doesn't have time this weekend.

Frank goes down to the basement and comes back with an old box of VHS tapes. It's like looking through a cache of childhood relics. They start going through the box, trying to find something unimportant that they can tape over without guilt.

"This one doesn't have a label."

"Play it. It might be blank."

Mr. Kirk sticks the tape into the VCR and hits play. I missed the whirring sound these machines make when they start up. There's a burst of static and white noise, and then...

"Turn around and smile! Wait, is the red light on?"

In the kitchen, a plate meets its untimely demise against

the tile. No one turns to look. Willa couldn't care less about it either. She comes and stands in the living room doorway, staring at the screen.

It's just an old family video taken at some beach, but Tessa is in it. She's behind the camera, telling everyone else to smile and greet the audience. The Kirks all lean in toward the TV like they're hearing a foreign language and are trying to decipher it. How long has it been since they heard Tessa's voice?

She turns the camera toward herself for a few seconds, waving into the lens. It's the first time I've seen a video recording of her. Tessa's face is alive and animated. She was young and healthy, a younger version of her mother.

The video cuts out, and after a burst of static, it shows footage of a high school track meet.

"Is there more of her?" Mrs. Kirk asks in a watery voice. Frank shrugs helplessly. "I haven't been able to watch our home videos in so long," she says mournfully.

Frank stops the tape and ejects it. "I kept all the old videos. They are more in the basement. You can take them back with you if you want."

Mrs. Kirk shakes her head. "I don't know."

I feel like an intruder on their grief. Every one of them has a faraway look in their eyes. Frank wraps an arm around Willa before I can, so I excuse myself to the kitchen. The broken glass needs to be swept up.

I notice a smear of pink on the tile. "Willa, did you cut your foot?"

Frank makes her sit down so he can check. Sure enough, there's a little piece of plate stuck in her heel.

"How did you not feel that?" he says.

"I was shocked." She didn't feel it when she cut her hand wide open the day Tessa died, either. While Frank goes to get tweezers, I wrap my arms around Willa's shoulders from behind and kiss her temple.

"I'm sorry, Hun."

"Do you ever look at your photo album anymore?" she asks.

"No."

We have equivalent scars in many tender places.

"No." Someday I'll look at the pictures Eric took, but right now, I can't stand the thought. Willa has had three times as long to recover from Tessa's death, but there's no limit on grief.

"Are you going to be all right?"

"Yeah, yeah. We'll be fine."

Willa sets a sixth place at the dinner table.

Interlude
September 2001

Frank

I'm counting on Tessa to be up late, and she doesn't disappoint. She turns into an insomniac when she's excited about something. Tomorrow she's off to St. John's University, and she's so pumped she probably won't sleep a wink.

Her room is already bare. Everything worth taking to school is crammed into two duffle bags. I find her at her desk with her feet propped up on the corner, doing something on the laptop Mom and Dad bought her for school.

"Hey. You got a sec?"

She looks at me over her shoulder. "Sure." She closes the laptop as I close the door. Mom and Dad are downstairs watching TV, but Willa is already in bed. We've got to keep it down.

"What's up?" She swivels her chair around

I take a seat on the bed. "I want to tell you something." At least, it seemed like a good idea in my head. Now that I'm actually face to face with Tessa, I'm not so sure I want to tell her anything.

"Did you break something of mine?"

"No, nothing like that." This simple denial must satisfy her. Tessa slouches lower in her chair and folds her hands over her stomach, as if she's settling in for a story.

"I'm… seeing someone."

"Anyone I know?"

"Yeah." Can we just leave it at that? Apparently not, because Tessa prompts me to continue with a circular hand gesture.

"Um…Doug?"

Tessa tips her head back and rolls her eyes. "Thank *God*."

"What?" Of all the possible responses I imagined, this was not on the list.

"I was worried you were going to put some poor girl through the humiliation of being your beard."

"My what?"

"Beard. Fake girlfriend."

"I…no. No, I'm with Doug." I add, "I'm gay." As an afterthought it sounds ridiculous. Would I be dating a guy if I weren't?

"I know."

She says it so casually, oblivious to what these words do to me. I feel slightly sick.

"How?'

Tessa shrugs. "You never seemed interested in girls, and sometimes you and Doug look at each other like you're doing that cheesy mind-reading thing that only people who are desperately in love do."

My face is on fire, and I think I might puke. "Shit. Do you think anyone else knows?"

Tessa puts her hand on the back of my head and forces it between my knees. Good idea.

"Dude, chill. You fly pretty low under the radar. If anyone does know, they must not think it's worth caring about, or they'd mention it."

That doesn't make me feel any better. I thought I was the one keeping a secret. How many people have been keeping it with me, too unsure or uncomfortable to say anything?

Tessa nudges my knee with her toe. "So who asked whom out?"

That's what she wants to talk about, of all things? "Neither of us. It sort of just… happened."

"You just read each other's minds?"

"No. We just sort of…fell in love."

"Well that's a boring-ass story."

I shouldn't snap at her, but I do. "My life isn't supposed to entertain you."

"This is a story you'll tell to future generations someday. So come on. How'd it happen? Who made the first move?"

Part of me wants to tell her about how wonderful it is, the rush of anticipation, the perfect sense of belonging. Then I think of the details of our day in the woods, and I don't want to relive them with anyone else. Those are just for Doug and me.

"Does it matter?"

"Sure it does. It's your history."

But it wouldn't mean the same things to anyone but Doug and me, so what's the point?

Tessa isn't giving up. "You've held hands?"

"Yes."

"Who reached out first?"

"I dunno." Now that it's something we do, I can't fathom why we didn't do it all along.

"Who leaned in to kiss first?"

"I don't want to talk about this."

"Come on," she whines. "Is he a good kisser?"

"Tess," I complain.

"What? It's not like I'm asking who pitches."

So this is what complete mortification feels like. "Goodnight." I practically leap off her bed but stop with my hand on the doorknob. "You won't say anything, right?" I only told Tessa because she's leaving home tomorrow. She can't give me shit about it after tonight.

"Of course not. It's your story to tell. You should work on telling it though. That was pretty weak."

I give her the finger, and she sends it right back at me.

"Get some sleep, loser."

12.
Granité

Willa

I feel a little shaky, but I don't want to let it show. Seeing that video of Tessa could have or maybe should have opened up a floodgate in this family. So far everybody is holding it together, so I have to do the same.

Everything in the kitchen is moving along right on schedule. The vegetables will be ready in twenty, and the potatoes are halfway done. The meat will need to rest a while, and the pie I made for dessert is cooling. Nothing needs my immediate attention, so I leave the kitchen in search of Jem.

He's upstairs using the bathroom. I slip in behind him and wrap my arms around his middle, resting my cheek on the flat between his shoulder blades. It's amazing how simply hugging him settles me.

"Um…I'm peeing."

"I'm aware."

He turns his head, trying to look at me over his shoulder. "You okay?"

"Yeah." I'm calm now, touching him.

"I'd hug you back, but…"

"I'm good." I kiss Jem between the shoulder blades. "I'll see you downstairs."

Frank is in the kitchen when I come downstairs, looking at the assembly of pots and pans like they're the inner workings of some complicated mechanism. "Uh, is there anything I can do?"

I give him something he can't possibly screw up. "Drain the broccoli?" He obliges, and insists I give him something else to do. It's almost time for dinner, for the Great Coming Out, and he seems nervous.

"I don't know. Want to polish forks?"

Frank gives me an irritated look. I lean in and lower my voice, so Mom and Dad can't overhear. "Relax, okay? Odds are they already know and just never said anything."

Frank lets out a tension-filled sigh. "It's the reason *why* they never said anything that makes me nervous."

"I'm pretty sure you'll still be the favorite child when this is over."

"Favorite is relative."

"Why must you shit all over everything when I try to be optimistic?" I poke him out of the way so I can reach the serving bowls.

Frank gladly picks one up and starts scooping glazed carrots into it.

"This looks really good." It's a decent attempt at a reconciliatory compliment, so I take it. "Jem's a lucky guy."

"I don't cook like this *all* the time."

Frank elbows me gently. "Hey, that promise ring...he didn't give it to you because he knocked you up, did he?"

It's such an abrupt change of subject that I have trouble coming up with a smart remark in time. "Because that's the only reason why straight people stay together."

"I'm serious."

"I'm not pregnant."

"Good." He nods with way too much enthusiasm. "I mean, someday it'll be great, but not when you're nineteen."

"I'm not entirely convinced that I'm the sort of person that should breed."

Frank frowns. "Why not?"

"Because my kids would have a chance of turning out like me."

My brother shakes his head, smirking, but I wasn't trying to be funny. What would I do if my kids turned out to be major fuck-ups like me? How could I lecture them without being a total hypocrite?

"You might be the last chance for continuing the family line," Frank says. "Don't write it off entirely."

"Don't write off surrogates," I retort quietly. That's all it takes to make Frank nervous and twitchy again.

"This was a bad idea."

Interlude
February 2004

Frank

It's late by the time I get to campus. Doug lets me into the dorm and we head upstairs to his room. His roommate is a local and goes back to his parents' house almost every weekend. It's a nice arrangement because Doug and I get the room to ourselves four times a month. I have to budget carefully to manage the cost of bus tickets, but it's worth it to be able to see him in person and touch him. And it keeps me feeling reasonably secure that he won't replace me with some pretentious fuck from McGill.

Doug flops down on the bed and stretches out while I take off my boots. "Your sister sent me a birthday card." He points to the shelf above his bed. The card has a picture of a beach at sunset on the front.

Dear Doug,
They really should have a greeting card category for "the guy who's doing your brother." This cheesy thing'll have to do. Try not to slip on the puddle of sentimentality.
Tess

I reread the first sentence three times. *The guy who's doing your brother.* God, is that how she thinks of Doug? And why would she write that on a birthday card?

"I shouldn't have told her. She isn't careful with other people's personal information."

Doug raises an eyebrow. "You mean secrets?"

He's out at school. I'm not. I used to think of my sexuality of a secret, but after coming out to Tessa I realized it was something different. It was nobody's damn business.

"No. A secret is something that *has* to stay private. Personal information is stuff you don't *want* to tell people because it's none of their business."

"I don't see the difference."

I sigh. Ever since he started Philosophy 101, he's been an argumentative knob. "The location of the corpse you had a hand in murdering is a secret. What you like to do in bed is personal information. See the difference?"

Doug rolls his eyes. "C'mere." He pulls me down beside him for a kiss. "Don't get bent out of shape. It's just a card. We have a weekend. That's it. Let's not waste it."

13.
Second Seating

Jem

There's a chorus of pot lids clanking and wooden spoons scraping that means it's close to dinnertime. I love the chaos that precedes mealtimes because Willa is always so proud when she times all the dishes correctly. I head to the kitchen to offer a hand, but I stop when I catch the phrase, "Why did you invite him?" Suddenly, I don't feel so welcome. If Frank doesn't want me here, I'll leave.

"Is everything all right?"

Frank practically jumps out of his skin. "Fine," he snaps.

Willa looks up from the roasted sausages and grimaces apologetically. "I'm coming out," she says lowly.

For a second, I think she means that Frank is planning to come out, but no. She said *I'm* coming out, as in she is the one who will be stepping out of the closet.

"Did you forget to tell me something?"

"Coming out by proxy," she amends.

"Oh…huh?"

"I'm using my status as least-favorite child to deliver information that might make Mom and Dad uncomfortable."

"I think you misunderstand the meaning of *by proxy*."

The withering look she gives me says that this is not the

best time to talk about it. I'm tempted to slide past this moment with a 'yes, dear.'

She turns to Frank. "If Doug can't make it tonight, I'll tell them tomorrow."

"Yeah, good idea," he says hastily.

The guy is desperate to put off the conversation, it seems.

Willa thrusts bowls of vegetables and potatoes into our hands. "Put these on the table. Mom! Dad! Dinner's ready!"

I've heard that it's a good sign when a dinner table lacks conversation. It means the food is so good that people don't want to pause for a second to speak when they could be eating. For the first ten minutes, no one says a word. We lay into the glazed carrots and rosemary roasted potatoes, the bacon sausages and broccoli, the green beans fried in garlic and soy sauce.

The first time any of us speaks, it's to ask that a dish be passed to the other end of the table. No one asks for salt; the food is seasoned perfectly.

"Save room for peanut butter pie," Willa says.

"You're not saving that for Thanksgiving Sunday?" Mrs. Kirk asks.

"I made a double batch."

Frank smiles like he's just been given the best news in the world. After dinner, he divides the pie while I help Mrs. Kirk load the dishwasher. His first piece is gone before we sit back down, and he serves himself a second.

"It's perfect," he says to Willa around a full mouth.

She hands him a napkin.

"Anyone want tea?" Mr. Kirk asks.

With the meal out of the way, everyone starts to relax. We're food-drunk and satisfied, and conversation starts to flow again. Mugs are distributed, and Mr. Kirk sets down a pot of mint tea. It's all very relaxing until Mr. Kirk looks at his watch and remarks that *Sixty Minutes* is going to start soon.

He gets up and takes his mug with him. "Frank, you coming?"

Frank shakes his head. "I need to be alone with this pie."

Everyone laughs, but I'm pretty sure he's serious. Dude's had two pieces already and shows no signs of stopping.

Mr. and Mrs. Kirk go to the living room, and Willa goes to the kitchen with the last plate of leftovers. I pour myself another mug of tea.

"Do you want me to go too?"

Frank shakes his head. "I didn't mean *alone* alone. Jeez." There's about half a pie left. I don't think it'll survive until midnight.

Frank props his feet up on the opposite chair and glances toward the kitchen. Willa is preoccupied, scraping pans.

"That's a nice ring you gave Willa," he says quietly.

"Oh. Thanks."

Frank shrugs one shoulder. "All right, so the pigeon thing is kind of weird, but the thought is nice."

I'm never going to stop hearing about *the pigeon thing*, am I?

Frank pitches his voice down even further. "I was also kind of worried that you gave it to her because you guys had some *interesting news*."

I have no idea what he's talking about.

"That's a small-town euphemism for pregnancy," he explains.

"Oh. No, she's not pregnant."

"I know. She told me."

"What did she say?" Now Frank is looking at me like I'm a liar.

I hasten to add, "I don't even know if she wants kids someday."

That is a lie. We both do it occasionally—make casual references to the things we'll do with our hypothetical children at some future date.

"No one wants kids at nineteen," Frank says dismissively.

That's not comforting. Most people *do* want kids at some point after nineteen. I glance at the kitchen door. Willa is still preoccupied with some loud task involving aluminum foil.

"I don't know if we'll be able to have kids."

He nods understandingly. "Because of the treatment?"

"Yeah."

Frank shrugs. "There are other ways. Cross that bridge when you get to it." He points at me with his fork. "And don't get lax about birth control in the meantime."

"Yessir."

Then we enter some parallel universe where Frank offers me advice on getting cheap condoms by buying in bulk. Apparently, you can get them in crates of five hundred or more. The fact that he knows that is a little disturbing. How much sex is he having? How much sex does he think *we* have?

"Um, I…. Thanks."

"Why so uncomfortable? You do *use* condoms, right?"

His tone makes it clear that there is only one right answer to this question. "Yes."

He grunts in approval. Then he makes me want to bleach my brain by adding: "Use them even if you're doing stuff that won't get her pregnant. Bladder and prostate infections aren't pretty."

I wonder if I can get away with telling him to shut up in his own house, because this conversation needs to end. Right the fuck now.

Frank reaches for a third piece of pie. How nice, that *his* appetite isn't affected by mental images of genital infections. I can barely sip my tea with that thought in my head.

Frank gives me a probing look and does this weird, circular nod. "You've been feeling all right?"

It's like he knows. Maybe he does. Maybe that's *why* he's giving me a hard time and it has nothing to do with Willa's promise ring.

"No."

In all fairness, if it were my sister's boyfriend in this situation, I would be pretty nervous for her and irrationally angry at him for making her feel insecure. So I can't blame Frank for getting a little stern and demanding the details.

"I passed out in class last week."

He goes into paramedic mode. "Dizzy spells? How's your blood pressure?"

"I was dizzy right before it happened. One minute I was sitting in class, the next I was on the floor with people standing over me."

"Did you hit your head?"

"They did a CT. No damage. I pushed up my annual blood tests."

"And?"

"Haven't heard back yet."

Dad was on the phone all afternoon, trying to use his connections to get my lab results back faster. I don't know why he bothered. He's got a snowball's chance in hell of getting lab work back on a holiday weekend, connections notwithstanding.

Frank sighs. He glances at the kitchen door, where Willa has finally finished wrestling with the tin foil. "She didn't say anything. Typical."

"She doesn't know."

He looks at me like I just grew a second head. "Don't keep secrets about serious shit like this, man."

The corner of my mouth twitches. "I'll pay you a hundred and fifty bucks to tell her."

Frank doesn't flinch. "You don't have that kind of money." He's right about that. "Did you give her the ring before or after?"

I mumble my answer, but he catches it anyway. Frank doesn't have to say anything. The look on his face is enough.

"It's probably nothing." That's why it's not a big deal that I didn't tell Willa. And she never has to know that I bought the ring right after because the timing would taint the gesture.

"Healthy nineteen-year-olds don't just pass out at random."

"Really?"

He jabs his fork at me again. "Don't be a smart ass."

Willa returns from the kitchen and pours herself a cup of tea. "Did you know that Lexapro makes most of the world's eyeglasses?" she says.

"Sixty Minutes?"

"Yep. I never needed to know that, but now I do."

I put an arm around her and pass the sugar bowl. I kiss her temple out of habit, and Frank narrows his eyes at me. This is a very PDA-averse family.

"Sorry."

"Hey," Willa says to Frank, "if we clink our cutlery on the glasses tomorrow, will you and Doug kiss for us?"

He blushes like a sunburnt lobster. That settles it. Forced kissing is a go. Too bad I won't get to witness the spectacle firsthand.

Interlude
May 2008

Tessa

It's one of those rare May days that feel like June, sunny and hot, with low humidity and no breeze. Mom is on the porch with her book, and I drag myself out of the house to join her. It takes a ridiculous amount of effort to prop my feet up on the porch rail. I've been retaining fluid, and my abdomen is slightly swollen. That can't be good.

"What are you reading?"

"Oh, you know," she says, which means it's a trashy romance. Mom has a weakness for bodice-rippers. "Do you need anything?"

"Not a thing." No pills, no injections, no medicated lotions. I'm not hungry or thirsty, and my pain is manageable. For the moment, I can just be me.

"I talked to Frank." Mom places her bookmark and sets the book aside. "He's going to try to come up for Victoria Day."

"Nice. Maybe he can take Willa to Confederation Hill." I won't be in any shape to celebrate, but it would be good for everyone else to get out of the house. Be normal for a while.

"We won't make any firm plans," Mom says tolerantly. "We'll just play it by ear. I told him he's welcome to bring a guest."

I'm not sure where she thinks we can fit Frank *and* a guest in this house, but it's a nice sentiment.

"Is he seeing somebody?"

I'm not sure how much Mom knows, and I never know what to say where Frank is concerned.

"He doesn't seem lonely," is her vague reply.

Great.

"But he's only twenty-four. It's important not to get tied down too young."

That almost makes me laugh. Frank and Doug have been pretty much tied down to each other since they were sixteen years old. To the casual observer, they look like best friends, but there are subtle clues that there's something more going on.

"I hope he decides to have children," Mom continues. "He was such a beautiful baby. Those big blue eyes…"

This is getting awkward. I promised him that I wouldn't say anything, but that was seven years ago. I thought he'd have come out to the whole family by now. I'm running out of time to say important things, so I go for it.

"You know Frank is gay, right?"

Mom snorts in amusement. "Well, I didn't think it was some *girl* leaving size-twelve footprints on his windowsill every weekend."

That sneaky bastard. I'm almost proud of my little brother, except for the fact that he was dumb enough to get caught.

Mom turns to me, eyebrows tilted in a tender expression of concern. "Has he said anything to you?"

"A long time ago when I still lived at home. He hasn't said much about it since."

"I read this book that said I should create a positive, welcoming environment, so he would feel comfortable coming out...but he never said anything. I didn't want to ask him because you know Frank. He can be so defensive if you push him."

"I know."

"He worries me. If he can go this long without saying anything to me, what else does he feel like he can't talk about?"

I mull that one over. Frank is the kind of guy who would sever his own hand before he asked for help, but I don't think he's keeping quiet about his sexuality because he *can't* talk about it. I think he doesn't *want* to, and my brother is a difficult man to motivate when he doesn't want to do something.

"Give him a little more time. I'm sure he'll have some great stories for you when he's ready."

14.
Petits Fours

Willa

Mom and Dad will be sleeping in the master bedroom. Frank will be taking my bed, at my insistence, and I'll be crashing on the couch. When I pitched this plan, Frank narrowed his eyes and asked if I had plans to sneak out.

"No, but if I was being that obvious about it, it would be sneaking, would it?"

Frank doesn't like rhetorical questions. Such wit and cleverness are totally unappreciated in this family.

Frank brings the empty pie plate into the kitchen just as I'm about to turn off the lights and go to bed.

"You are going to be so sick tomorrow."

"Shut up," he whines. I take the pie plate and set it to soak in the sink. "God, I'd be five hundred pounds if you still lived here."

"Don't exaggerate."

"You know all my weaknesses too. Chocolate pie and roast potatoes..."

"Doug doesn't know you're a slut for pie? After eleven years?"

Frank rolls his eyes. "I don't think sluts are this secretive about their desires."

"Good point." I smirk. "Y'know, Tessa and I had this deep philosophical conversation about the word slut once. She didn't want me to say it because she thought it was unfair to condemn other women like that."

Franks snorts and shakes his head. "Of course she did. But you would have been too young to remember...."

"What?"

"Tessa was a slut in high school."

I don't have many qualms about speaking ill of the dead, but Frank is the only person who could say that about Tessa and not pay dearly for the privilege.

"She had a lot of boyfriends. That doesn't make her a slut."

"I used to steal condoms from her all the time."

"Owning condoms does not make her a slut, either." She could have been a serial monogamist or owned them and never used them.

Frank quirks his eyebrow. "Owning them in multiple sizes?"

There's a long, uncomfortable pause. "Damn it. Okay, fine, she might have been a slut."

"I know more about these things than you do." Frank pats my head like I'm five. "You still believed in Santa Claus when she was out parking with that buck-toothed numb nuts from the 7-Eleven."

"The dude who smells like onions?"

"Yup."

"Jesus." That dude *still* works there as far as I know.

"She didn't have the most refined taste at seventeen. Or any taste, come to think of it." Frank shrugs. "Buck-toothed onion guy still gives me free gum sometimes though."

"*That's* the benefit of having a slutty sister? Free gum?"

"Yeah. I just wish she'd fucked my mechanic instead. I could've used free oil changes."

I try to punch Frank in the shoulder but he dodges my fist. "You are such an asshole."

"Wrong. An asshole would have suggested that *you* get me free oil changes."

"Sorry, reformed slut."

Frank shakes his head and reaches for the kitchen light. "I don't understand how you two could sleep with more than one person. Just can't wrap my head around it."

The bulb goes out, and the only remaining light comes from the stairwell.

"It was just skin. It wasn't meaningful before," I tell him through the darkness. "Have you really only ever slept with Doug?"

Frank makes a noise that sounds like agreement. His socked feet brush softly against the tiles as he heads for the door.

"Then how can you be sure he's the one for you?" I think I would at least be *curious* about sex with other people if I'd only ever had one partner.

There's a smile in his voice when he says, "Do I seem unsure?"

"I guess not." He seems perfectly content, almost disgustingly so, whenever I'm allowed to glimpse the connection he has with Doug.

"G'night, Willa."

15.
Eighty-Six

Jem

Dad knocks on my door before bed. I set aside my laptop when he comes in and shuts the door behind him. This isn't going to be a casual, goodnight chat. He must have gotten some information back from the lab, and he doesn't look happy.

Dad takes a seat on the edge of my bed. I ask if we should wake Mom up for this conversation.

"No, no, she took a sleeping pill," he says dismissively.

Maybe the news isn't so bad. If it were truly a catastrophe, he would want her here too.

"Do you remember Dr. Wheeler?" he begins. "You met him at the Christmas party a few years back."

"Doesn't ring a bell." My parents' social circle contains a lot of doctors, obviously, but on top of that, I was introduced to a parade of people in white coats when I got sick. Names and faces start to run together after a while.

"He's a hematologist," Dad says. That's the only important bit, really, and he immediately moves on. "I got him to take a look at your tests. He was able to push them through the lab faster."

"And?"

"You didn't go vegetarian and neglect to tell me, right?"

"No. Why?"

"You're anemic." This has been a problem in the past, when I had cancer.

"Does that mean…?"

"Your cell counts are fine," he says firmly. "It looks like you just have low iron. We'll get you some supplements and see how things go. Your case isn't even that severe as far as these things go. Did you eat breakfast on the day you passed out?"

"Toast." I was running late, by which I mean I walked in fifteen minutes after the lecture started and the prof gave me a death glare.

Dad gives me a look that tells me I should know better. "Eat something real for every meal. And your supplements. Don't slack on those."

"And if I don't improve?"

Dad pats my knee. "You will. This isn't nearly as serious as it could have been. It's a good thing." He stands up and musses my hair. I'm about ten years too old for that. "Count your blessings, Son."

We exchange goodnights and he leaves, closing the door softly behind him.

"God," I sigh, and sink down into bed. I'm reluctant to feel relieved just yet, but some of the weight of the past week has been lifted off me.

I should tell Willa what happened. It's less daunting, now that I know I won't have to hurt her. I can't imagine how she would react if I relapsed. I can imagine the guilt of putting her through that though.

It's too late to call, so I send her a text: *I love you so much.*

Thank you for being mine.

16.
Offals

Willa

The light of the TV wakes me up. The back of the couch is mere inches from my nose, but that's definitely an electronic glow against the cushions. I roll over and find Mom on the opposite couch, watching the TV on mute. It's a home video of some long-ago Christmas. I wasn't even born yet, and Frank was pure baby fat.

I say, "Turn it up."

Mom startles. "I didn't mean to wake you." She sounds as if she has a bad head cold.

I pick up my blanket and join her on the other couch, draping the comforter over our legs. "What year was this?"

"1988, I think. We'd just bought a camcorder." Mom inches the volume up until we can just barely hear it.

"Frank, what did Santa bring you?" Dad asks.

Frank holds up a bucket of Duplo blocks and lets out a giggle that would be maniacal if he wasn't so damn cute.

"What are you going to build with those?"

"Wocket!" He opens the bin with fat little fists and proceeds to build a toddler's approximation of a rocket ship, ignoring all encouragement to come open his other presents.

So he was always that stubborn.

A few feet behind him, my five-year-old sister is getting excited about something Barbie-related. She'd already outgrown dolls by the time I was old enough to play with them, so it's weird to see her get worked up about a Barbie.

"I was an accident, wasn't I?"

Why else would the age gap be so big? Tessa was nine and a half when I was born. Frank was seven.

"No," Mom breathes. "I missed having a baby in the house. Frank and Tessa were in school, so I thought we'd try for another. I wanted two more."

"What happened?"

Mom shrugs. "After you, nothing. Nature has its ways of letting you know when to be happy with what you already have." She reaches over and finds my hand under the blanket.

It's so strange, to be touched by her again.

"You were lonely a lot when you were little, weren't you?"

"Not a lot." There are definite benefits to being the baby of the family, and those outweigh the times when I felt left out or hopelessly far behind. "Sometimes it kind of felt like being an only child." I thought of my siblings as adults for most of my childhood. They were never my peers. Without really thinking about it I blurt out, "I think two kids would be a good number. Maybe three."

Mom turns to me with a gentle look of surprise. "Do you think you and Jem will have children? I know he went through a lot of treatment."

"I have no idea. Honestly, I haven't spent much time thinking about the specifics."

Mom nods. "You're young. You're not supposed to think about these things yet." She squeezes my hand. I squeeze back. I didn't realize how much I missed touching her, and I've got a feeling that she'll accept whatever grandchildren we bring her, whether they're biologically ours or adopted.

"Was'dat?" Toddler Frank finally loses interest in his blocks and scurries over to Tessa, who has just unwrapped a Ken doll.

Frank's eyes go wide, and he presses his hand against the plastic of the box, as if he's just discovered that boy dolls exist.

"He ripped the head off that doll," Mom says. "Tessa was so upset."

"I bet."

"We got him a G.I. Joe a little while after this, but he didn't play with it as much as Tessa's Ken doll."

That's extremely telling. I look over at Mom, absorbed in the antics of her young children. She smiles warmly, but a tear makes its way down her cheek every few seconds. This feels like the moment. It's our first heart-to-heart in years that hasn't included any resentment or blame. So I go for it.

"You know Frank is gay, right?"

I expected her to get a little emotional, but when her breath hitches and she bursts into tears, I know I'm out of my depth. "Aw, shit." I try to hug her.

She sobs, "Why do I have to hear this from everyone but him?"

"You mean you *did* know?"

"Of course I knew. I'm his mother." She reaches for a tissue, but the box is empty, so she wipes her eyes on the sleeve of her housecoat. "Tessa said he came out to her. Why would he come out to her but not to me?"

Oh. So she knew about that. I rush to defend Frank, but I

really didn't expect the conversation to go this route. All my plans and arguments are moot.

"Because…because Tessa was his peer. He could afford not to care what she thought of him. And he told her the night before she moved out. He knew she wouldn't have the chance to prolong the conversation."

"Really?" She hiccups.

"I don't think it has anything to do with you. It's just Frank being Frank, you know?"

Her sleeves are getting pretty wet, so I offer her mine. She laughs. It eases the tension, and I feel bad for having to test her limits again, but Frank did pay me.

"There's something else you should know."

"What?"

"This is Doug's couch."

She smiles tenderly. "They're living together now?"

"Yep." I nod slowly. "Because they're married."

I've got to hand it to Mom—she reacts better than I did.

"Married? How long have they been dating?" She sounds more concerned than indignant.

"Eleven years."

She laughs. It's a disbelieving laugh, but full of relief. "That's Frank. When he finds something he likes, he doesn't let go."

"Fuckin' right, eh?"

Mom gives me a look. "Language."

"Sorry."

"Married…" She says it like the word is new to her and she's trying to wrap her mind around the very concept. "When did they get married?"

"Just last month. I'm still pis…*annoyed* that he didn't invite us."

"Are there pictures?"

"Just *one*."

Mom purses her lips. "That boy."

Toddler Frank bounces on screen, declaring in a baby's lisp that he has to go potty. The tape cuts out, and when the image resumes, it's Easter. We're a family that only pulls out the camera on holidays. It's another early morning, and Tessa and Frank are on an egg hunt in the backyard.

"Why the backyard?" There's evidence of shitty, Canadian April weather all over the place, with hunks of snow and slush, icicles on the swing set, mud everywhere…

"Because if they didn't find all the eggs, the *remainders* wouldn't stink up the house."

"Ah. Fair point."

Mom nods to the screen. "He would have met Doug just a few months after this. They went to the same preschool."

"I thought you had to pull Frank out of preschool?"

In the video, he looks angelic and stubby in his snowsuit, blond curls peeking out from under his toque. But that kid used to have a real issue with biting other children. The preschool teacher told Mom that he just wasn't ready for school yet.

"I did," she agrees. "Funny thing is, Doug and Frank didn't get along there. A year later in kindergarten, they were best friends." She shrugs. "Children, eh?"

"Did Frank stop biting?"

"Mostly." She smiles. "When I was the age Frank is now, I'd only known your dad for two years. Can you imagine, knowing the person you're in love with since the age of four? They've had more than twenty years to get to know each other."

"And they're still not bored of each other," I add. It's kind of amazing, when you think of it like that.

"They've got true love," Mom says kindly. "The mate-for-life type like swans or geese."

"Or pigeons."

Mom gives me a funny look but doesn't comment. After a while, she says, "I think you and Jem have that too. You can see it in the way couples look at each other. It's obvious which ones connect on the deepest level."

I'm touched, but I don't know what to say. I settle for, "Thanks." But that feels inadequate and dumb.

Mom squeezes my hand again. "I don't doubt you two. You've been through hard times together already. You'll be fine with whatever else life throws at you."

That's exactly why I trust Jem's affection so much, because he loved me even when love was anything but easy. He could have walked away without blame or guilt, but he stuck it out with me. That's how I know it's real.

The video of Easter morning ends with a sugar-induced meltdown and skips ahead to Victoria Day. It looks like this was shot at the park. Tessa has cotton candy dye all over her face and is trying to explain, what the holiday a five-year-old's logic. She describes the fireworks that will happen at night and holds her arms wide and announces, *"Daddy got a BIG box of beer!"*

Toddler Frank turns to Tessa and asks, *"Where beer?"*

"Beer is a grown-up drink," Mom informs him from behind the camera. *"Not for little boys and girls."*

Frank starts crying like she just told him that Santa Claus isn't real.

"God, this family is weird."

Mom chuckles. "Hey, he turned out okay in the end."

Maybe I should warn Frank that I came out for him before Mom has a chance to ambush him at breakfast. I told him I would do it tomorrow when Doug is here too, and he's probably not going to like it that I deviated from our plan.

I say I have to pee and head upstairs to use the bathroom at the top of the landing. Frank's bedroom door is closed, and I open it very slowly, feeling like the murderer from *The Telltale Heart.* Frank is sound asleep, snoring like a wildebeest. Maybe I ought to roll him over before he swallows his tongue. Is that even possible?

I sit down on the edge of the bed, but he doesn't stir. So I poke him in the shoulder, and keep doing it until he jolts awake with a loud snort.

"Shhh."

"W'time is it?"

I look at the clock on the nightstand. "Three. But that's not important. I told Mom."

"M'what?" He's not compxletely awake yet.

"I came out to Mom for you." *That* wakes him up.

Frank looks at the clock again, like it might be lying, and then back at me. "*Now?* You told her now?"

"We were watching home videos from when you and Tessa were babies, and she seemed...I dunno, emotionally primed? So I went for it."

There's a long pause where he just stares at me. Frank makes a puppeteer motion with his hand. "It sounds like logic when you say it, yet it makes no sense."

I'm going to pretend that the ungrateful bastard didn't just insult me.

"Dude, she already knew. And she's cool with it. I mean, she's pissed that you only have *one* wedding photo, but that's not a big deal. She said you and Doug are, like, perfect for each other."

"She did?"

"Well, there was a bird metaphor involved."

Frank blinks in bewilderment, and dismisses my remark. "What about Dad?"

"Still asleep. I'm pretty sure Mom will tell him when he wakes up." I think that kind of open information sharing is called 'parenting.' "If Mom knew all along, Dad probably did too. You're pretty much in the clear. Except for the whole secret wedding bullshit. They're gonna skin you alive for that."

Frank lets out a disbelieving little chuckle. "Can't believe I slept through my own coming out," he murmurs.

"Convenient, isn't it?"

Frank pulls me down for a hug, tucking my head under his chin. It's an uncomfortably tight hug, and after a few seconds, his breath catches.

Fuck, he's crying.

I don't want to move. I know that he's having a well-deserved *moment*, probably full of some complex emotion that I will never understand as a straight person. I don't know how to comfort him without making him feel like pansy, so I play possum and let him sniffle into my hair for a few minutes.

After a while, he realizes how tight he's gripping me and his arms relax a little. "Sorry."

"You sound like a frog." That wrenches a smile out of him. I offer him the sleeve of my hoodie, and he wipes his face on it.

"Is she still up?"

"Yeah."

I know I should probably mind my own business and let them have their moment, but I'm a nosey fucker. I crawl out to the landing to watch Frank head downstairs. The glow from the TV dims just as he reaches the ground floor. I can't see into the living room from here, so I crab-walk down the stairs like a creep, trying to keep quiet.

"Hey," Mom says quietly.

That's the last thing I hear. They're totally silent. I can't tell if it's a good silence, or if one of them is smothering the other with a pillow. I peek around the corner for a look. They're hugging like people who have been apart for many years. I suppose secrets and silence create an entirely different form of distance.

Mom looks over Frank's shoulder and sees me peering around the doorjamb, so I do the awkward thing and give her a thumbs-up.

Mom loosens her hold on Frank. "We were just watching home videos." She clears her throat and sniffles a little. "Do you want to watch with us?"

Mom changes the tape. I make tea. Frank spreads the comforter across everyone's laps, and we watch a more recent video. I was actually alive for this one.

"I think you were five, here," Mom says.

It was suppertime, but I can't figure out what the occasion was. Maybe someone was celebrating a birthday. We were in the backyard of the house I grew up in, sitting around a patio table. Dad was grilling, and a bunch of my siblings' friends were there. Doug and Frank are just visible in the background, kicking around a soccer ball.

I think one of Tessa's friends shot the video, because the camera stays close to the table where her group was sitting. They laugh at inside jokes that none of us get now. I bet if Tessa were still alive, she wouldn't even be able to explain them to us.

Mom isn't in this video, but I was off to the side, blowing bubbles.

"See," Frank says, "you used to be normal once."

"Shut up."

Five-year-old me abandons the bubbles and approaches Tessa. *"I'm thirsty."*

She looks at me like she has no idea where I came from. *"What'cha gonna do for it?"*

Her friends toss out suggestions, and they settle on a recitation of "I'm a Little Teapot." Five-year-old me complies without batting an eye, doing the actions with complete abandon.

"You were so easily influenced when you were little," Mom says. "It's a wonder you're so strong-willed now."

On the screen, Tessa hands young me a plastic cup and tells me I've earned it.

"Better than being a pushover." I don't think I'm strong willed. I get through things because I have to, but I get exhausted. I still allow others to influence me—case and point, my reluctant association with Jem. I'm not as strong as everybody thinks I am. I just throw my weight around when I have to.

Five-year-old me spits the red drink all over the place.

"This tastes like markers!"

Tessa sniffs the cup as she mops up the mess with napkins, and her eyes go wide. *"Oops. Wrong one. Let's uh, get you some milk."*

Frank laughs, and even Mom chuckles a little.

"She gave me alcohol?"

"She used to get vodka from 7-Eleven guy," Frank says.

Mom hums disapprovingly. "I wondered. She was always causing trouble at that age."

I wonder how I could have lived in the same house and been so oblivious to it all. I suppose it was the innocence of childhood that kept me from seeing her as anything other than perfect.

Mom turns away from the TV to look at me. "Was it her idea or yours?"

"To give me vodka?" What five-year-old wants hard liquor?

Mom gives me a good long look, and I know exactly what we're talking about. The thing we *don't* talk about.

"Hers." But it was my fault for going along with it…for being so easily led. "We didn't know if it was just another setback or the end. She panicked. I panicked."

"That's why you locked the door? To make sure no one could help her?"

There's a tone of calmness in the question to which I am totally unaccustomed. We have never discussed Tessa's death at this decibel level. Maybe Mom practiced talking about it in therapy.

"She was beyond help, Mom." I didn't want to give Tessa the pills when she asked for them because she was already so pale. Another five minutes, and she would have bled out anyway. But Tessa insisted on pills. She wanted to be sure that this was the end of her torment.

"It's not about help," Mom says. "It's about comfort."

There's no arguing that there are more comfortable, dignified ways to die than lying naked on a bathroom floor.

"We panicked." That's really the only explanation I can offer. We were scared and made bad decisions, thinking only of the moment and forgetting the big picture.

Mom says something that sounds like, "I wanted to hold her."

Frank puts his arm around her, and I pass her another tissue.

Interlude
August 2008

Frank

It's late, almost one o'clock in the morning, so I take a cab to my parents' house. When I get there I stand on the sidewalk for a moment, debating whether to call that cab back and go to a hotel instead. The house looks so anonymous, so run-down, as if people who have had disaster blow through their lives live here. I don't want to be that family.

I shoulder my bag and go inside, letting myself in with the spare key, because we *are* that family.

The house is quiet, but someone left the hall light on for me and the couch is made up for sleeping. I'm tired, and I don't feel like company. I go right to sleep without even bothering to change.

Dad wakes me up. "You were supposed to call," he says.

I stretch carefully. My back is already starting to cramp from being on this couch. "I got in later than expected. Didn't want to wake you."

He nods. "You hungry?"

"What time is it?"

"Almost ten."

I can't believe it. For one, I'm too tired. For another, the house is too quiet. The light coming through the drapes is wan, as if the sun is still struggling to rise.

"Really?"

Dad goes to the kitchen. "I'll make eggs."

I get up to take a piss, still half-asleep. It doesn't occur to me until I'm ready to leave the bathroom that Tessa died in one. Was it this bathroom? How many bathrooms are in this bungalow? Christ, did she die right where I was peeing?

I don't want to ask Dad. I'd rather avoid the subject of death altogether. He hands me a plate of scrambled eggs.

"Where're Mom and Willa?"

"Your mom has been sleeping a lot," he says. "Willa, too. She hurt her hand. The painkillers make her sleepy." He sets his own plate down on the table and turns to more business-like topics. "The service is at two o'clock. We have to be there for one o'clock to take care of any last-minute details. Did you bring a suit?"

"Yeah."

He nods. "If your mother isn't up by noon, I'll drive over at one by myself, and you can bring the girls along at two."

"All right," I say, though I'm horrified at the thought of managing my distraught mother. I don't do well with crying people, least of all her. Mother's tears are frightening.

At eleven, I go in to wake up Willa. I could use an ally in dealing with Mom, who is still in bed. Every few minutes, I can hear sobs coming from behind her door. Dad, who is even worse at this stuff than me, has escaped the house under the pretense of washing the car. Mom wants to grieve loudly, but he just wants to grieve alone.

Willa is still in bed, tangled in a light blanket and facing the wall. Her bedroom looks like a hostel room, with all the beat-up furniture. It's clear that she's been living out of a laundry basket in the corner. All I see are shoes and dirty clothes.

"Hey." I nudge her shoulder.

Willa grunts.

"It's time to get up."

"Later."

"Now." I pull back her blanket.

She's curled protectively around her bandaged hand. I want to ask how that happened and how recently, but I'm concerned with the appearance of the bandage. There's a long yellow stain on it. The gauze looks grimy and the edges are frayed.

I pick up her wrist, causing Willa to hiss. "When was the last time you changed this?"

"I dunno."

I keep one hand on her wrist to steady it and use the other arm to lever her out of bed. I walk her down the hall to the bathroom of death and sit her down on the toilet lid.

"Do you have any…" I find the first aid kit under the sink and start digging for scissors, fresh gauze, and tape.

Willa groans and wipes her eyes. "What time is it?"

"Eleven." It doesn't look like midday in summer. Tessa was always bragging about the nice sunny days here, but so far the weather has been nothing but weird.

"Put your hand on the counter."

Willa lays her wrist out, and I cut away the gauze. It's thickly wrapped around the middle of her hand to support her thumb, which is held close to her palm. Before I even have the gauze off, the smell is apparent. The skin is infected.

"Jesus Christ." Under that bandage is a long line of stitches, and the skin around them is a dangerous shade of purple. It's swollen around the sutures and pus is seeping out, yellow in some places and green in others. "When did this happen?"

"Couple days ago," Willa says. "I'm not sure what day it is."

"Thursday." *The day of our sister's fucking funeral,* I want to add. I open the vanity drawers, looking for something to mark with. I find some sort of makeup pencil and draw a line on Willa's wrist where the inflammation ends. I wrap her hand loosely in gauze. "We're going to the hospital."

"I'll just put Polysporon in it."

"You will not." I have to take her back to her room like a stubborn toddler and force her to put clothes on.

Dad is still washing the car when we come out of the house.

"I'm taking Willa to the hospital."

He shuts off the hose. "Why? What's wrong?"

"She let her hand get infected."

She cradles it close to her chest as if she's afraid I'll make her show it to Dad.

"It's almost noon…"

"We'll be there for the service." I don't think we will. But there's nothing more that can be done for Tessa, and Willa needs me.

We're kept in the waiting room at Emergency for three hours before anyone sees Willa. The doctor takes one look at her hand and decides that the stitching will need to be removed to clean out the necrotic tissue. Willa changes into a hospital gown while we wait another forty minutes for a surgical consult. She asks me to help her tie the strings at the back. When did she get so skinny? I can count her ribs.

The surgeon is a woman, fast-talking and bluntly analytical. "The muscles that control your thumb will probably be severely damaged," she says. "I'm not so sure we'll be able to save the thumb at all."

For some reason, this doesn't faze Willa.

I wait with her until they take her in for surgery, and then I'm booted to the waiting room. I'm not used to hanging around in places like this. My typical day consists of dropping people off at the ER and going right back to the ambulance.

I call Dad, but his cell is off, so I figure he's still at the wake. I find it odd that he hasn't called yet, either to nag us for being late or to find out what's going on with Willa. Once crisis at a time, I suppose.

I've stopped looking at the clock by the time Doug enters the waiting room, still dressed in the suit he wore to Tessa's funeral.

"Hey. Your flight was okay?" I can't bear to ask him about the other thing.

"Yeah, fine." He sits down and takes my hand. "How is she?"

"I dunno. It's all so fucked up."

His thumb strokes mine. I can tell he wants to hug me, but I can't stand to be touched right now. I'm just looking for a reason to hit something.

"I can postpone my return flight."

"No." I shake my head. "Go. I've got this."

I'd rather know that one part of my life, the part that has him in it, is functioning in a normal and familiar way. I need return to him in three days and find that everything is the same… or as close to the same as possible.

It's well past dinner hour by the time they let me see Willa again. She's lying in the recovery ward, staring at the ceiling and giving monosyllabic answers to the intern asking about her pain level.

"Be helpful," I tell her.

"It's a yes-or-no question," she insists.

Her hand is wrapped in a partial cast. It has plaster on the underside to keep her wrist and thumb steady, and is held on by layers of cotton and tensor bandage.

"She'll have to come back in two days. We'll clean the wound and give her a bandage she can remove herself," the intern says.

I want to talk to the attending, but Willa's problem is relatively minor, and I don't want to be a pain in the ass.

"Do you live with her?" the intern asks.

"Uh, no."

"Make sure you speak to whoever she lives with about keeping the wound clean. It needs to be dressed and cleansed on a regular basis to prevent infection. When she comes back we'll also show her some exercises for that thumb. It'll never be the same, but if she doesn't exercise it and the scar heals too tightly, she'll be worse off."

Something about the way he says it makes me think he's just regurgitating whatever his supervisor said to him.

"Do you have any questions?"

"When can I take her home?"

The intern looks at his watch. "Eight. Maybe nine."

Willa mutters something very rude under her breath. I scold her for it, even though I end up saying the same thing an hour later when I see how much an afternoon of parking cost me.

I tap on Willa's window. "You got any quarters?"

"No."

"How about a twenty?"

She gives me that look—the one Tessa used to give me right before she called me a lame ass or a dork or a spazz. Credit card it is.

I haven't eaten since breakfast, so I stop at Wendy's on the way home. Willa insists that she doesn't want anything. I get her a frosty anyway. She needs *something*, and it's a one-handed food.

"How fucked up do you think my hand will be, really?" she says as she bites the wrapper off the plastic spoon.

"Watch your mouth."

"Fuck off."

"Don't talk to me like that—I just wasted an entire day in the hospital with you. You could have lost the thumb, kid."

Willa lifts her cast and looks at the bulky bandage. "I guess I'll have to postpone my dream of being a streetwalker, huh?"

Was that a joke? She's *joking* at a time like this?

"I tell you that you almost lost a very important digit, and you make a crack about giving *hand jobs*?"

Willa rolls her eyes. "Right. You're Frank. Boring and draconian."

"Where's this smart mouth coming from?"

"I had it installed when I hit puberty."

"Well, switch it off right this minute. I don't need your attitude right now."

"Eat your burger. You're being a cranky bitch."

I take my food three tables away so that I'm not tempted to strangle her. Of all the ways today could have gone horribly, this was not one I had imagined. I would rather have given the eulogy naked. Doug is good at dealing with this crap, but I'm not. He's got a talent for emotional crises, probably because his family has so many. I like the kind of crises I can stop with bandages and IVs.

Willa gives me just enough time to finish my burger before she comes over and taps me on the shoulder.

"What?"

"What time is it?"

Isn't there a goddamned clock in here? I check my watch. "Ten."

"The funeral was at two."

"I know."

Willa slides into the seat across from me. She looks genuinely worried, which is a first today. I suggest that we swing by the cemetery, but Willa shakes her head.

"She wasn't buried."

I didn't know they were planning to cremate Tessa until we get home and my big sister, or what's left of her, is sitting in a white urn *on the fucking coffee table*. They left her there like a goddamn vase.

I pick her…it, up and put it…where? I settle for the mantle. Place of honor, right? "This is so messed up."

Willa snorts. "Like you have any idea."

Mom comes in and her eyes go right to the coffee table. She goes from zero to shrill in half a second. "Where is she?"

"I put her on the mantle."

"That's not a trophy, Frank!"

Dad's after her to calm down, talking as if he's dealing with a mental patient. Mom snatches the urn off the mantle and cradles it close to her chest like a teddy bear. She's crying again. Or maybe she never stopped.

"Where were you?" she screams at me. "You fly all this way for a funeral and then you don't even…"

I have to shout over her to tell them where we've been, that Willa's hand got infected and she needed another surgery. They removed ligament and muscle and her thumb is now permanently damaged. I thought I had a handle on the whole thing, but Mom is still shouting at me for skipping the funeral.

Dad is trying to make her let go of the urn before she drops it and the words just come out. "Why the fuck weren't you watching her? Another day and she'd have been fucking septic!"

Mom sobs, and Dad begins to tear up. I turn to Willa and realize that the person I was just gesturing to isn't standing there. She heads out the front door so fast that all I see is a flash of blonde curls.

"Wait!" I catch up with Willa halfway down the driveway and grab her arm. "You can't take off. You're in no shape to…"

"Fuck off!" She jerks her elbow up and hits my jaw.

Dad opens the screen door so roughly that he nearly takes it off its hinges. "Both of you get back in here *now*!"

Willa has no intention of listening to him any more than she does to me. I grab her around the waist and try to haul her back up the front walk, but she hits me again—deliberately this time.

Dad is losing it. "Stop acting like jackasses and *move it*!"

Willa is stronger than she looks. As I lay on the wet front lawn where I've fallen on my ass, blood pooling on the inside of my lip, it occurs to me. We've become that white-trash family that fights on the front lawn.

17.
Amuse Bouche

Willa

Dad finds the three of us asleep on the couch the next morning, curled up under the same blanket. "What are you all doing down here?"

Mom stretches, blinking owlishly. I try to slump down and steal a few more minutes of sleep.

"We were watching old videos," she says around a yawn. "And talking."

I expect her to roll right into the fact that Frank and Doug are married or bring up the subject of Tessa's death for the umpteenth time. But she just stands up and rolls her shoulders, working out the kinks.

"I might need a nap later. Anybody want coffee?"

"Yes," I mumble.

Frank agrees too. I smile at him, and he shakes his head.

"You already blew my health kick."

"It's unnatural, refusing coffee."

Frank pulls the blanket closer and drops his head down to one of the throw pillows. "I don't want to hear about it until I've had at least one cup."

We're just sitting down to breakfast when Doug comes home. His eyes are a little bloodshot.

"You hung over?" I ask as he hugs my mother hello.

"I'm *dehydrated*," he says with great dignity.

Frank puts on the kettle to make that herbal tea Doug likes.

"I didn't know you were coming over this morning." Dad goes to the cupboard for an extra plate.

Doug and Frank share a meaningful look. Dad doesn't know that Doug lives here, and now Doug knows that Frank pussied out about telling them.

Doug tucks into pumpkin waffles on Dad's left, and we all try to pretend that life is normal. Frank hands Doug a mug of something that smells like grass, and their fingers brush for a second. It must be hard, not to be able to greet each other intimately after enjoying the freedom that living together provides. When Frank sits down, he places his foot over Doug's. I'm no romantic, but damn, that's sweet.

We're out of chairs, so I hop up on the counter and balance my plate on my knees.

"These are good, Willa," Doug says of the waffles. He smirks. "You didn't use whole wheat flour, did you?" He's trying to get a rise out of me.

"No, you hippie, I used Bisquick. Eat your bleached-flour, capitalist flapjacks."

"Don't be rude," Dad says, oblivious to the joke.

Mom changes the subject to window washing, of all things, and Frank agrees that he should do it before winter comes.

"You should paint before it gets too cold. So you can open the windows to vent the fumes." Dad turns to Doug and says, "You gonna help him finally paint this place?" Dad's trying to be chummy, but the awkwardness is palpable.

"Of course," Doug says smoothly.

I nudge the back of Frank's chair with my foot. "What do you think, ivory or cream?"

Everyone laughs except for Frank.

Mom suggests cactus green for the living room. "It's a calm color, but masculine."

Frank shrugs and replies that green is green.

Mom is undeterred. She continues, "Oh, and then you could paint the front hall a nice shade of taupe. It would match the tile."

I think Mom truly believes the tile is beige. It's actually just in need of a mop. Doug agrees that taupe could work for the upper and lower hallways. I don't know much about paint, but I can't resist.

"I hear couples with caramel-colored bedrooms have more, um…romance."

There's a pause where Dad seems to be deciding whether to choke at the mention of sex. He turns to look at Frank and says, "Are you seeing someone?" in a tone of complete surprise.

Frank's shoulders tense up beneath his t-shirt, and I know he's going to give some wishy-washy non-answer. So I start singing Wagner's March.

"Dum, dum, dum, dum…"

Dad sets his fork down, like holding it marks the line between distraction and undivided attention. "You're getting *married?*"

Mom smiles at Doug across the table.

"He's already married," I interject before Frank can answer.

Dad sputters. "To whom?"

I make a sweeping gesture to Doug.

At the same time he says, "Um, me." He does a good job of sounding meek. Maybe that'll keep Dad from losing his shit completely.

Mom tries to smooth things over. "We should toast to you two," she says, reaching for her coffee mug.

Dad is staring at Doug with his mouth open, as if he's seeing him for the first time.

Mom is the only one to raise her mug. "To the newlyweds."

"Cheers!" Turns out I can't compensate for the awkward silence with added volume.

Dad turns to Frank, still looking stunned. "When did you get married?"

"Right after Labor Day."

"This year?"

"Yeah." There's silence for a few beats before Frank adds, "We just went down to the courthouse. It wasn't a big deal."

"Not a big deal," Dad repeats.

Mom reaches for Frank's hand. "Of course it's a big deal. It's your wedding."

Dad pushes his chair back with a loud scrape. "Excuse me."

No one tries to stop him from leaving the room, but when he leaves the house altogether, we all look at each other in askance. Doug reaches for Frank's hand.

"Think he'll be okay?" I ask Mom.

"He thinks better when he has time alone," she says. "He'll be fine."

18.
Juiced

Jem

"Do we have to spray the pan first?" Elise wonders aloud.

We've figured out that it will take about five hours to roast the turkey, but that's the least of our problems. I set the laptop on the kitchen island while Elise cuts the packaging off the turkey.

"Maybe you should do that in the sink," I say, a second too late. Fluid leaks out all over the counter, and I have to lift the laptop up to avoid the flood.

"Ah, crap." Elise scrambles for a towel. She shoves the turkey into the sink and starts mopping up the salmonella.

"Should we bleach the counter?"

"Before or after we finish handling the food?"

We stare at each other for a beat. "Flip a coin?"

Eric comes in just as we're trying to figure out how to clean the bird. First, we have to establish which is the ass end, and I try to hold it up while Elise pulls the neck out. The cold skin is slippery and hard to grip.

"This is so gross," Elise says, elbow deep in turkey butt. She pulls out the neck with a great yank, and a piece of fat flies up to land on her cheek.

"Eeeeeww!"

Eric backs out of the kitchen slowly. "I'll just, um…bye."

The bastard could at least peel carrots.

We rinse the turkey, pat it dry, and set it in the roasting pan. It's beginning to feel like we're accomplishing something, but Elise has to go and point out, "Wait, aren't we supposed to stuff it?"

I hang my head. "Shit."

"I'll Google it."

While Elise researches recipes for stuffing, I text Willa. I'm a little ashamed to admit that it just took us forty-five minutes to clean a turkey, so I try to bring the subject around slowly.

Sleep well?

It's almost noon; she should be up and active by now.

Willa replies: *Stayed up and had a touchy-feely movie night with mum and Frank.*

I completely forget about the turkey for a moment. Willa isn't close enough with her mom to do touchy-feely *anything* on a regular basis, but if Frank was involved, I can guess the reason.

Does she know yet?

She knew all along. Pissed that he got married and didn't tell her, tho.

I read that text several times, but that doesn't make it less shocking. *He's married??*

Welcome to the inner circle.

"Well?" Elise interrupts.

"What?"

"What did she say? Does she have a recipe?"

"Um…I'll ask." I get an eye-roll from Elise before she turns back to the laptop.

I need a favor. What's your stuffing recipe?

It takes Willa a long time to type her reply, and when I see it my heart sinks. The first ingredient is two loaves of bread.

"We don't have bread, do we?" I ask Elise.

"In the freezer, *maybe*." She gets up to check. "No bread, but we've got frozen croissants and a leftover bagel."

I scan through the rest of Willa's recipe. I'm pretty sure we have almost everything else to make stuffing.

"Okay, those'll do."

"You think?"

"You got any better ideas?"

19.
Appetizer

Willa

I put the turkey in the oven at noon and get all my other prep out of the way before two. Vegetables are sliced, butter is portioned, and the dishwasher is running. I feel so accomplished, but I'm the only one.

Frank has been sulky, which makes me feel guilty, especially because Doug seems to be cool with what happened at breakfast. He's in the living room with Mom, chatting about mutual friends. I believe in a town this small that's called 'gossip.'

"Do you feel like you got your money's worth?" I ask Frank as I set a timer on the turkey.

He shrugs.

"I'm sorry. I should have put more planning into it…or tact."

Frank ignores the apology. "Where do you think Dad went?"

He walked out three hours ago, and we haven't heard or seen him since. Nothing is open on Thanksgiving Sunday, so where could he possibly go?

I suggest that he might have just gone for a walk. That doesn't seem to comfort Frank any.

"I used to imagine him getting mad," he says. "I didn't think he'd just stare and then walk out."

"Well, he can't yell at you like when you were a kid any-more." I give my brother a hug and assure him that Dad will be back in time for dinner—hopefully with a clear head and his frustration pre-vented.

My phone buzzes in my shirt pocket, and Frank takes a step back to let me answer it. I've got another text from Jem.

What does the breast part look like? I think I've got it upside-down.

"The fuck?" Frank says.

"He's talking about the turkey."

"Oh. Jesus. I mean…good."

"Jem knows what human breasts look like."

Frank shudders. "I can't deal with this," he mutters and stalks away.

20.
Table d'hôte

Jem

The turkey is finally in the oven. We're both covered in butter and blood (some of it ours), but the turkey is in the damn oven, and that's all that matters. Mom comes into the kitchen as we're setting the timer and offers to peel carrots. Elise and I look at each other with dread. We still need side dishes. Fuck me.

"Let's just order pizza," Elise says.

"Sides are easy," Mom insists. She lists them on her fingers. "Boiled carrots, steamed peas, mashed potatoes, and yams with marshmallow. That's it, right?"

"Okay."

Elise calls dibs on the peas.

"That's the easiest thing. They're *frozen*."

She puts her hands on her hips and glares me down. "Excuse me, who had to repeatedly shove a hand up the dead bird's ass?"

"Enough," Mom interjects. "You peel potatoes," she points to me. "Elise, you peel carrots. I'll peel yams."

We go to the fridge and pantry, and the cycle of defeat starts again. We have just two carrots, no yams, and the potatoes have gone horribly soft. Little tuber-y legs sprout from each potato like something out of a horror movie. The ones at the bottom of the sack are black, semi-liquid lumps.

Mom steels herself with a sigh. "This is not hopeless. We can have non-traditional sides." She grabs a can of beans off the pantry shelf and holds it out to me. "We can microwave these, and…uh…help me out here."

This will forever be known as the Thanksgiving we had beans, ramen noodles, and scrambled eggs.

21.
Entrées

Willa

I try not to be obvious about watching the front window for Dad's return, but I think Frank is on to me. With the drapes open, the neighbors can probably see me watching the front lawn. Does this look creepy?

The flag on the mailbox is up.

"Did you forget to check your mail?" I ask Frank.

"It's probably junk," he says.

I go out to check, disbelieving that anyone would waste the long weekend distributing junk mail. Frank is indeed correct. The postal service is closed today and tomorrow, but three different parishes decided to stuff the mailbox with flyers for their holiday services and autumn pasta suppers. Mom and Dad met at one of those. I guess that's an indication of how little there is to do in this town.

I'm about to crumple the flyers when I feel a set of eyes on me. It's the next-door neighbor, standing near the back hatch of her minivan with a laundry basket full of casserole dishes.

"You should come," she says, gesturing to one of the colored flyers. "It's always a great night."

I smile at the potential zealot and nod. "Thanks." Now I

probably have to wait until I go inside to destroy the flyer…

"You should tell your brother to come," she continues.

Did I do anything to invite conversation? Jesus…

"One of our pastors has had a lot of success with people like him."

For a moment, I'm stunned. I didn't think people were so upfront about their prejudices anymore. Hasn't political correctness shamed everyone into silence yet?

I crumple the flyer in my hand. "Has he had any success curing bigotry?"

"Homosexuality is a sin," she says, suddenly not to friendly. Then she hisses, "And this is a family neighborhood."

"So what the fuck are you doing here, ruining it for everyone?"

"Does your mother know you talk like that?"

"What my mother knows is irrelevant, and you can take your religion and shove it up your fat pasty ass." I give her the finger, huck the ball of flyers onto her lawn, and march home. I slam the door behind me for good measure.

"Jesus, Will, take it off the hinges, why don't you?" Frank shouts from the kitchen. I stomp in there, full of righteous indignation, and announce, "Your neighbor is a cunt."

Frank doesn't even blink. "The fat soccer mom?"

"Yeah."

"Yep." He nods, not at all fazed by the bigotry of someone who lives within brick-throwing distance. It occurs to me that for all Frank's a quiet guy, he's got a handle on his shit.

"How did you get to be so put together?" Honestly, I should probably be closer to 'functional adulthood' by now. Maybe there's a secret I'm missing, a chapter of the manual I didn't read.

Frank lets out a great snort. "What are you talking about? I can't even be bothered to paint my walls. And if Doug hadn't moved in when you left, I'd have gone back to eating frozen burritos and pizza all the time."

"See, *that's* what makes me wonder why you're not five hundred pounds."

Frank shrugs. "Good genes?"

"I heard a door slam." Doug comes up from the basement with Mom. He was showing her the birdhouses he makes in his spare time. Honestly, I didn't know Doug had so many weird hobbies until this weekend.

"Mrs. Linsky tried to save our souls again."

"Ah." Doug smiles like it's an old joke. "Did you tell her you already spend enough time on your knees?"

Mom reaches up and smacks Doug on the back of the head like he's her own son. Welcome to the family, indeed.

"Don't be inappropriate," she scolds.

"Sorry, Mrs. K."

"Call me Mom," she says, like nothing happened. She turns to Frank and me and asks if Dad is back yet.

"Nah." Frank shakes his head.

"We should take bets on where he went," I suggest. Everyone ignores me.

"Honestly, I'm embarrassed," Mom says. She takes the kettle to the sink and fills it.

I hope Doug has non-grassy tea around here...

"It's childish and hurtful, to storm out like that. No wonder you were reluctant to come out."

Frank's shoulders start to curl inward, protecting himself against a threat only he perceives. "It wasn't your fault or anything," he insists.

"We could have done better by you. I can understand being reluctant to come out. You didn't know how we'd react, and you were still dependent on us for such a long time."

Frank's dependency was his choice, though. He could have moved out after college, but he lived with Mom and Dad until Tessa got sick and they sold the house.

Mom turns to Doug and asks if he's out to his family.

"I came out in college."

Her eyes widen in surprise. "They never said anything to us either."

Doug shrugs. "It wasn't really their place to do that."

"I suppose you're right." She opens the cupboard and starts rummaging for tea. "But good for you, telling them so young."

My phone buzzes with another text from Jem.

Scrambled eggs only take 5 mins to make, right?

I don't even want to know.

Mom goes out to pick up Oma at four. Dinner is scheduled for five. Dad is still on his 'walk.' I lean over to give the turkey its final baste, and Doug has the balls to ask me how much butter I used on this thing.

"You're twenty-seven years old. Your heart and arteries are *fine.*"

"Are they teaching you about alternatives to butter at that school?"

I straighten up and brandish the baster at him. "Keep talking and I'll cover the turkey in cheese just to spite you."

Frank smiles dreamily, as though he's fantasizing about cheesy turkey.

The front door flies open with a slam. Oma enters the house yelling, "Hello!" at the top of her lungs. "Where are the newlyweds?" she hollers. Oma isn't deaf; she just likes people to think she is so they'll discuss delicate topics in her presence.

She takes Frank's face between her weathered hands and plants a big, sloppy kiss on his cheek. Then, because we all have to take a turn being indignant, she scolds him as only Oma can.

"I didn't even know you were dating. I could have set you up with Gloria's son. You remember Gloria? From my poker game?"

Oma doesn't wait for an answer before she plops down in the easy chair. "Come over to my house sometime this week, and I'll give you my china. I was saving it for your wedding gift."

Frank tries to beg off. "You don't have to do that, Oma. Really, we don't need…"

"No one *needs* china. It's your problem now." She turns to Mom and says she can't even remember the last time she used the good china.

I duck into the kitchen and muffle my giggles while Frank tries to put on a polite expression of gladness.

"Just you wait," he says when he comes to get a drink for Oma. "I bet she's saving something equally useless for you."

God, I hope it's not her collection of Hummel figurines…

Thanksgiving dinner is almost ready. I set up the food mill to whip the mashed potatoes (the fact that Frank even owns one of these must be Doug's influence) while the boys set the table. Oma joins me in the kitchen just as I'm scooping fluffy mash into a serving bowl.

"And where's your man tonight?" she demands.

"Jem's with his family." I don't know that he'll enjoy being there though. Last I heard from him, he was asking if it was possible to burn ramen noodles. I have no idea why he would be cooking ramen on Thanksgiving, but I've got a feeling this is one of those things better left unquestioned.

"Let me help you with that." Oma takes the hand mixer and starts to disassemble it. She drops her glasses in the sink and says, "Aw *fuckshitdamn*. Willa, pass me a towel."

I hand her a dishcloth. Her face looks so much smaller without a set of giant frames in front of it.

"Do you think I've got time for a smoke before dinner?"

"You've got thirty minutes while the turkey rests."

"Perfect." She turns around and cranks it up to pseudo-deaf volume. "Hen! Come join me on the porch!"

I try to take the turkey out of the oven quietly. Non-foodies don't seem to grasp the fact that meat needs to rest, and they'll flock to the table like seagulls if they think the turkey is ready right this minute. I scoop out the stuffing and get my carving knife and fork ready. This turkey looks pretty damn perfect, if I do say so myself.

The side door opens and closes quietly. Who was out in the garage? I lean around the kitchen doorframe and find Dad standing there, shrugging out of his windbreaker.

"You're just in time. Dinner's almost ready."

That seems like a safe thing to say. He probably saw Mom and Oma on the front porch, and circled around the garage to avoid a scolding.

"Smells good," he says gruffly. Dad clears his throat and

tries again, more jovial this time. "I'm sure this is going to be a great dinner."

He offers to call everyone to the table, but I tell him I need a few more minutes to carve and plate the turkey. Dad studies the bird admiringly for a few seconds.

"Nicely browned," Dad says as he reaches for the carving knife. "Want some help?"

I would rather carve myself, but today has been rough on him, so I accept his help. Maybe being involved in the meal prep will improve his overall mood.

But then he starts cutting the breast without removing the wings first, and my hands itch.

"Actually, you should start with the legs. Cut here and then separate the hip joint." I point to the meat between the body and the leg.

Dad glares at me. "You think you know everything, don't you?" His tone is way more hostile than this situation demands.

A few years ago, I would have snapped right back at him, but I'm *reformed* now. Got to keep calm.

"We're not talking about everything. We're talking about carving a turkey."

Dad throws down the knife and carving fork. "I don't know why I bother. You kids are so determined to shove us out of your lives."

"Eh?"

He's already out the back door, stomping around the makeshift patio as if someone just pissed in his cornflakes. I'm going to take a wild guess that this isn't about turkey carving technique and pin it on Frank's decision to elope.

"Need help?" Frank passes through the kitchen to grab

wine out of the fridge and nods at the turkey.

"How do you manage to still be the favorite child even when you fuck up?"

He blinks in surprise. "What did I miss?"

I point to Dad through the kitchen window. He's blown off a little steam by pacing and is now staring at the birdhouse like it's personally responsible for all his problems.

"Apparently we're shoving him out of our lives. Like, for example, by not inviting him to your freakin' wedding."

"When did he get home?"

"Five minutes ago. Does it matter?"

Frank ignores the question. "I'll go talk to him."

The turkey is ready for carving, but it can stand to sit for a few more minutes. I inch the window open a crack and lean over the sink to eavesdrop.

"You were gone a while." Frank manages to comment on this without sounding judgmental.

I don't know how he does it. I wouldn't be able to resist the urge to question where Dad went.

"I don't want you to think this is about you being gay," Dad says firmly. "Because it's not. I've known that since you were a little kid." He doesn't look at Frank, but he keeps one hand on his hip and makes that flat-handed, authoritative gesture that he used to do when we were little and he had to give us shit. "But there are proper ways to do things, Frank," he says, voice rising. "You invite your family to your wedding, goddamnit. You *tell* them you're getting married."

"Lots of couples elope," Frank says patiently.

"Don't give me that shit. You didn't elope. You planned this and deliberately excluded your family."

"It's not like that."

"It's exactly like that," Dad snaps. "After everything this family has been through, you would shut us out and make a secret out of the most important day of your life."

"It wasn't a secret."

"Really? What was I supposed to do, check your fucking Facebook page?" Dad turns away again and swears.

Frank offers to do a vow renewal ceremony at a time that's convenient for Mom and Dad, and Dad barks at him that he's missing the point.

"You cannot continue to shut us out, Frank. We've already lost Tess, and you break this family up even more by shoving us away. At least Willa bothers to *call* every once in a while. I have no idea what's going on with *you*, and if I ask, you don't tell me." He throws his hands up in frustration. "I don't know what to do with you. Honestly, I don't."

Frank doesn't even try to defend his behavior. He just stands there, hands in his pockets, looking contrite. I wonder if Dad's going to buy that.

"When were you going to tell us you were married?" Dad says. His voice is almost level, but the calm is fragile.

"This weekend. It's why I invited everyone here for Thanksgiving." He shrugs. "I didn't know how it would go, after Christmas…"

That was the last time our family was all in one place. The holiday consisted of three days of screaming matches and taking sides.

Dad looks away, shaking his head. "It's always a fight, isn't it?" he says sadly. "Things should have been different."

His real meaning is in his tone. *Things would be different if Tessa had never gotten sick.*

Frank nods in the direction of the back door. "Can we try

to have a normal family dinner?"

That won't fix anything, but it's a step in the right direction.

Dad doesn't answer for a few seconds, but then he looks at Frank and smiles. "With Oma around? Normal is relative, Son."

He's trying, and a profound sense of relief fills me. I can't imagine how Frank feels right now, being at the center of all the tension and watching Dad let it go.

"Come on." Dad directs Frank toward the back door. "Let's go help your sister. Apparently I've been carving a turkey wrong for the last thirty years."

22.
Fine Dining

Jem

I think I can safely say that this is the worst Thanksgiving dinner ever conceived. The turkey is as dry as firewood, and the carrots aren't cooked evenly. Elise burnt the ramen, so the noodles have random crunchy bits. I'm not sure about the stuffing. It's kind of mushy, but it smells like it should. We attempted gravy, and Elise disposed of that culinary corpse by dumping if off the back porch. We couldn't risk it coming back to life and crawling up the kitchen drain. The scrambled eggs turned out okay, thankfully.

Everyone looks either bummed or apprehensive except for Elise, who is embarrassed. She invited her boyfriend for Thanksgiving dinner, and he gets to eat this massacre instead.

Dad suggests that we take turns sharing what we're thankful for. Good idea. We can avoid eating for a few more minutes.

"I'm thankful that we're all together this weekend," he says.

Sure, pick the easy one.

Eric is thankful that midterms are over. Mom is thankful that we worked together on this meal with minimal fighting.

Elise is thankful for the nice weather—a cop-out if I ever heard one. Her boyfriend is thankful that the government has decided to close a nuclear plant in Quebec.

"I thought you said his *parents* were hippies?" Eric says to Elise.

"Eric," Dad interjects. He manages to make Eric's name sound like *shut up, Boy.*

"What are you thankful for?" Mom prompts me.

"I'm thankful for Dad's connections."

Mom slides an extra slice of turkey onto my plate. She smiles as though she's glad I have a problem that can be easily fixed, for once.

"Dig in," Dad announces. "First one to choke has to do the dishes."

23.
Aperitif

Willa

The year Tessa died, we didn't celebrate Thanksgiving. None of us had the emotional energy. In the year that followed, holidays were occasions to get plastered and yell at each other. My last Thanksgiving at home was the worst because the family was already making plans to ship me off. This Thanksgiving, everyone is blessedly normal. No one gets drunk—not even Oma—and there's a distinct lack of name-calling, shaming, and crying. It's like we all made breakthroughs in therapy and forgot to notify each other.

Frank makes coffee to go with dessert, the second peanut butter pie, and Doug doesn't even object. Mom and Dad start to clear the serving dishes away, and as soon as they're in the other room, Oma turns to me.

"Grab my jacket, Love," she says. She reaches into her pocket and pulls out a joint. And it's not even Canada Day. I love my grandma.

"We're gonna go get some air," I call to Mom and Dad.

Turns out Oma brought enough pot for everybody. Frank and Doug join us on the back patio and Oma passes around two more joints.

"None of you carry lighters?" she scolds when we all have

to use hers. "You should always carry a lighter, even if you don't smoke. You meet interesting people that way." Oma takes a long drag and holds it in, savoring it. "It's also handy if you have to burn evidence," she says, smiling mischievously.

Sometimes I wonder if she's actually done half the stuff in her stories, or if she puts it on to keep people interested. That must be one of the shittier parts of getting old, the way people think you're less and less relevant over time.

The sliding door opens and Mom steps out, wrapping her jacket around herself. There's no point trying to hide the pot, but Frank tucks his hand behind his hip anyway.

"Yeah, I know what *going out for some air* means." She plucks the joint out of my hand. Mom takes a short pull and holds it in.

"You're not on medication, are you?" I ask as I accept the joint back. Not that my memory is very clear, but I seem to recall that antidepressants and pot don't mix well.

"I'll be fine," she says, polite but terse, and goes to grab a lawn chair.

24.
Check, Please

Jem

Mom agrees to loan me her car on one condition. I have to drive Kipp home first. Normally, the thought of doing that guy any favors would bug me, but being alone in a car with him doesn't seem so bad. It'll give us a chance to talk.

"Elise looked nice tonight, eh?" I say as I back out of the driveway.

Kipp nods.

I award zero points for such a non-committal agreement. "I'm kind of surprised she wears that much makeup," I continue. "She never used to do that."

"It's been a rough school year for her," Kipp says.

Points for an honest answer, and bonus points for telling me something about Elise that I didn't know. "Really? It's only October."

"The transition out of high school has kind of made her anxious. She's been on edge a lot."

"But she's smart." Elise was never top of the class or anything, but she was a solid honor roll student for all four years of high school.

"You don't have to be dumb to be scared of failing." He gives me this shifty look, as if he's afraid to look me in the eye. "And she doesn't, uh, have her usual support system."

Points for not leveling a direct accusation. Both Eric and I took off to school this fall, and Elise picked a local college. She's used to having her brothers around, and since my illness we've been closer than ever. Elise lost all that in the space of a week, and yes, I feel like an asshole about it.

"I should call her more."

"That would be good."

He's so polite and passive, it's annoying.

"She's been hanging out with a new group of friends." Kipp shrugs uncomfortably. "I don't really like them, to be honest."

"Why not?"

"One of them's kind of a burnout," he says. "And she's been hanging out with this girl who parties a lot. But she puts Elise down, like, every day."

I thought my sister was smarter than that. I guess I have to respect the way Kipp shows concern for her well-being and the bad influence her friends have over her, but I also want to blame him for not protecting her.

"Have you suggested that she hang out with other people?"

Kipp snorts. "You can imagine how well that went over." He knows my sister very well, it seems.

"Dude, you're local," I tell him. "I'm not. I can call, but I can't protect her when I'm an hour and a half away. If she's in a bad place, or headed for one, *help her*."

I expect more than a silent nod in response, but that's all Kipp gives me. I can't tell if he's socially awkward or trying to annoy me on purpose.

I turn off onto his street and stop in front of the house with an NDP banner and a "Stop Harper!" sign on the front lawn.

"How'd you know this was my place?"

I smile. I guess that means he's socially awkward, if he doesn't know that the political posters, rock garden, and plethora of wind chimes give this place away as a hippie haven.

"Lucky guess."

"Thanks for the ride."

He gets out of the car, but I call his name before he shuts the door. Kipp bends down to look at me.

"I'll support you, whatever you do to help her, okay? You've got my number."

"Uh, no, I don't."

I can't resist rolling my eyes. "Elise has it programmed on her phone."

Kipp pulls his phone out of his pocket. "I don't know if she'll give it to me if I ask."

I take his phone with a sigh. "You haven't ever hacked your girlfriend's phone? That's, like, Dating 101."

He gives me a weird look. It's almost the exact same look Willa gave me the first time I broke into her phone to add my number.

I hand Kipp's phone back. "I'll see you around."

"Okay." He smiles awkwardly, but there's genuine gratefulness there. "Thanks."

"Thanks for not being a complete douche to my sister."

"I would never…" I hold up a hand to cut him off.

"Shut up. You're human. Don't make promises you can't keep." I put the car in reverse and Kipp closes the door. I roll down the passenger window to tell him one last thing. "But Kipp…"

"Yeah?"

"I promise to break your legs if you ever hurt her."

"I know. Eric keeps sending me videos of attack dog training."

You know, once in a blue moon Eric has a truly genius idea. I wish I'd thought of that.

"Excellent."

I head straight to Willa's house after dropping off Latham. No one answers the door when I knock, but there's noise coming from the backyard, so I circle around to the garage gate. The whole family is out in the backyard, singing a drinking song in what sounds like Dutch. Willa's grandma is leading the chorus, holding a joint overhead like a conductor's baton. I can smell the weed from the far side of the garage. It appears that Willa is having a better family holiday than me, for once. It's about time; she was due for one.

The song ends as I sit down on a vacant lawn chair. Willa starts whistling, and Frank picks up the tune. They start clapping their hands and singing "On Top of the World" by Imagine Dragons. One of the neighbors yells at them to shut up.

Willa turns and hollers, "Get fucked, bitch!" She claps a hand over her mouth and giggles like she can't believe she said that.

The rest of them roar with laughter like it's the funniest thing anyone has ever done.

"I'll call the police!" the neighbor yells back shrilly.

Willa starts singing "Fat Bottomed Girls" at the top of her lungs, and everybody else joins the warbling choir.

Jesus, how long have they been out here smoking?

Willa's grandmother turns to me and says hello. "I don't know who the hell you are," she says with such sweetness.

"I'm Jem, Willa's boyfriend." I've met her grandmother before, but I looked quite different then, and she was sober.

"Oh," she says warmly, and reaches out. It looks like she's going for the old lady cheek pinch, but she pets my hair instead. I just go with it.

Willa sidles over and takes a seat on my lap. "How was your dinner?"

"Today, I'm most thankful that you can cook, because I certainly can't." I kiss her cheek and she laughs.

"There are leftovers in the fridge if you want 'em."

"Thanks."

I'll grab a plate in a little while. Right now, I just want to enjoy having Willa on my lap. She offers me a toke, but I decline.

"By the way," I say lowly, "my bloodwork showed I'm anemic." It's not a bad thing to tell her when she's stoned, right?

Willa giggles. "Are you just trying to get attention?" she jokes.

"Nope. Completely serious."

"Okay. I'll cook more red meat." She's too relaxed to worry, and I'm glad. The gravity of the situation will occur to her later, when she realizes that I just dodged a bullet. I'm safe. We're safe.

"Thanks." I tuck my hands into her jacket pockets and hold her close. Our bodies fit together perfectly, like aligning pieces of a puzzle. "This is home," I murmur.

Willa smiles and reaches back, tracing a finger along my jaw. She makes a pigeon coo with her mouth. "Forever and unconditionally."

Author's Notes

Some of you may be happy to hear that bacon sausage is a real thing. I bought some last summer at Sasloves Meat Market in the Byward Market of Ottawa. It's absolutely amazing with dijon mustard and pickle.

Just like with *Wake*, the recipes mentioned herein are available on my website. Stop by to say hi and browse the catalogue of recipes if you're interested.

Acknowledgements

Books are not written in vacuums, and this one would have never seen the light of day without the generous support and talent of many people.

Thanks and warmest regards to Su Ah Chu for brilliant edits and copyediting expertise.

The food in Love Among Pigeons would not be so rich, detailed, or delicious if not for the help of Dan Fachin. Thanks for brainstorming recipes with me, putting together fictional menus, and for going to Cordon Bleu in the first place. Oh, and thanks for feeding me. Can't forget that.

Shannon from the blog Twilight Sleep, you can die happy now. Thanks for giving this book such an enthusiastic early response.

Thank you to my early readers for your feedback, support, and flailing excitement. Your comments were invaluable.

Lastly, thank you to everyone who took the time to read and respond to this book. Writing is a lonely profession at times, but you make it worthwhile.

About the Author

Abria Mattina works in marketing, writes to stay sane (or maintain a particular level of insanity, depending on your perspective), and blogs about books for fun. When she isn't doing any of those things, she's probably baking.

Visit her at www.abriamattina.com